I
Am
the
Clay

I
Am
the
Clay

❖ ❖ ❖

CHAIM
POTOK

ALFRED A. KNOPF
New York
1992

THIS IS A BORZOI BOOK
PUBLISHED BY ALFRED A. KNOPF, INC.

Library of Congress Cataloging-in-Publication Data

Potok, Chaim.
    I am the clay / Chaim Potok.—1st ed.
      p. cm.
    ISBN 0-679-41195-X
    1. Korean War, 1950–1953—Fiction. I. Title.
  PS3566.O69I15 1992
  813'.54—dc20   91-58550
                                                        CIP

Manufactured in the United States of America

First Edition

A number of people were of considerable help to me in the research for this book: Millicent and Mario Materassi of Florence, Italy; James Stovall of Haver-town, Pennsylvania; and Kyung-Ae Lim of Seoul, Korea. I offer them my deepest thanks.

—CHAIM POTOK

There is no sun without shadow, and it is essential to know the night.

—ALBERT CAMUS

BOOK
ONE

1

During the last retreat, when the Chinese and the army of the North swept down into the South, an old man and his wife fled from their village in the hills and embarked upon a panicky trek along the main road to Seoul and at one point scrambled with other refugees into a roadside ditch to avoid an approaching column of American tanks and jeeps. There they came upon the boy.

The old man glanced at the boy: blood-covered, barely breathing, lying face-up and unconscious in the snow in the bottom of the ditch. He looked indifferently away.

Two jet fighters swept past overhead, low. The steel-treaded thunder of the tanks; the trembling of the earth. Soil along both sides of the ditch cascaded upon the old man and the woman and the boy.

The old man thought matter-of-factly: This ditch will be my grave.

Shells exploded close by. A stench of cordite filled the air. Something moist and cold fell upon the old man's face. He reached up to brush it away and saw it was a hand and thought it was a hand of a body blown to pieces, and his skin crawled. But it was the hand of the boy.

Lying on his back in the ditch, his head in snow to his ears, the boy had waked to semi-consciousness.

The old man looked a long moment into the boy's dark beseeching eyes and spoke briefly to his wife.

She opened the boy's shirt and gazed at the wound: a shrapnel gash below the right collarbone, the sliver of metal showing darkly, the wound oozing blood. A piece of the scale from the dragon of death. Remove it.

The last of the tanks had gone. On the road now were American and Korean foot soldiers. The refugees began to climb from the ditch. Townspeople and farmers and villagers. From the valleys to the north. Possessions on shoulders and heads and in carts. Infants carried on the backs of older children. Old women straddling the backs of middle-aged men. All begrimed, terrified.

Two carts had been sideswiped by passing vehicles and men were lifting them out of the ditch. An ox lay dead in the ditch, still harnessed to its ruined cart. Vapor rose from its mouth and hindquarters. The old man could see no wound. Dead, how? The heart abruptly ceasing? He had seen it before: an ox plowing and suddenly faltering, lurching to its knees, and collapsing onto the furrowed earth. And the day the carpenter's younger brother lifted a house beam to his shoulder and fell lifeless to the ground. Alive one moment, the next moment dead. You can't help it.

The old man climbed out of the ditch. Their cart stood on the edge of the road, where they had left it. The bright sharp morning air was wind-whipped and bitter cold.

The woman remained in the ditch beside the boy. The man looked around. The once-frozen road had been ground to powder by the steel-cleated tracked vehicles. A cloud of yellow dust hung over it like a fog. On both sides of the road were terraced fields bordered by wild winter grass and tall hills. No human sounds came from the road: only the clanking scraping leathery noises of the marching men and the creaking of the two-wheeled carts and the occasional bellow of an ox.

The old man turned impatiently and called to the woman, but she would not move. The ditch lay deep and empty save for the woman and the boy and the tawny-skinned dead ox attached to its wrecked cart.

He called again to the woman. She looked up and down the empty ditch and then at her husband. She pointed to the boy, who had again lost consciousness and now lay with his head in her lap.

The man saw that her skirt was stained with the boy's blood and he began to shout at her in anger but his words were cut off by the sudden chop and beat of a helicopter swooping in from the south and flying so low he could see the pale helmeted face of the man inside. He put his hands to his ears. Air vibrated inside his throat and head. When he looked again at the ditch he saw his wife trying to climb out, carrying the boy.

Angry, he took the boy from her, and was momentarily thrown off balance by his lightness. Like a small bird. He laid him down on the pile of quilts in the cart. The woman made her own way out of the ditch.

He thought he would take some flesh from the dead ox. It would soon be stripped clean, why not take some part of it? One of the legs perhaps. But the woman was talking to him about the boy.

He looked at the dead ox. Two men were already cutting it with their knives. Left behind, why? Diseased? But one can burn away disease over an open fire. Abandon a dead ox. This war made people crazy.

The boy lay in the cart, on the quilts. The woman stood beside the cart wiping the filth of the ditch from his face and looking at the sliver of metal embedded in his chest. The wound seemed deep, the flesh inflamed. She remembered hearing from the carpenter that such wounds should quickly be brought to one skilled in hospital medicine. She leaned over the side of the cart, trying to stanch the flow of blood with cloth she had torn from her skirt.

The old man took up the shafts of the cart and moved into the line of refugees. Her eyes upon the boy, the woman walked alongside the cart.

As they passed the ox the old man saw five men now sundering it. Because of the boy he could take nothing from that ox. His own ox he had not brought with them, because he feared he could not feed it in flight; he had left it in the shed with an open sack of grain. He did not think it would live long or that their village would survive this attack. It was said the Chinese looted everything and what they could not carry away they burned. He and his wife in their haste to flee the village had taken only their quilts and sleeping pads and the box containing the spirit of his father and enough food to feed themselves for a few days.

Around a curve they went by an elderly man lying on his back on the side of the road. Eyes and mouth black holes. Dead a long time. The line of men and women and children moved imperturbably past him.

The old man walked as if hitched to the shafts of the cart. They would bring the boy to a hospital somewhere or to an orphanage and move on. Probably he would die first. Then they would leave him on the side of the road. The land was filled with orphans. They roamed the hills and valleys like packs of wild dogs, stealing, scavenging, plundering. Obstinate old woman. Why did they need now upon their backs the additional burden of a strange boy?

❖

The woman walked alongside the cart, feeling through the cloth she held to the wound the moist warmth of the boy's blood. He lay semi-conscious, burning with fever, and when he began to shake she tore more strips of cloth from her skirt and wrapped them around his chest—he stiffened as she moved him but did not cry out—and then put a quilt over him. She spoke briefly and silently to the spirit of her long-dead mother and to the spirit of the leafy chestnut tree near the veranda of her home in her childhood village and to the spirit of the only child she had borne, who had died in his first year of life. She traced in the air over the boy the long vertical and horizontal motions taught her by her mother to ward off the demons of death.

Pulling the shafts of the wagon, the old man heard the thump of distant artillery and tried to think only of each next step his feet must take on the torn and dusty road. The middle of the road was clogged with jeeps, trucks, and ambulances. On one side refugees fleeing south; on the other infantry in two lines moving north. Troops on the footpaths and in the frozen fields beyond both banks of the road, strung out in thin advancing lines all through the valley.

Two single-engine fighter planes approached from the south, about fifty feet above the ground. They followed the contours of the valley, vanished below the crests of the nearby range of hills, and reappeared on the other side as if launched from catapults.

The old man turned to his wife in time to see her step away from the cart directly into the path of an oncoming ambulance.

He stared at her in a paralysis of astonishment. All around him he heard shouts. He let the shafts of the cart fall from his hands.

The woman stood in the road. As the ambulance rolled

past him, the old man saw through the closed window of the cab the startled face of the Korean driver. He found his voice and shouted a warning to the woman. The ambulance braked to a halt in a swirl of gravel and dust.

There was a moment of silence. Behind the ambulance the long line of vehicles came to a halt.

The driver rolled down his window and put his head out. "You crazy? You want to become food for worms?"

The old woman pointed to the boy in the cart. "Hurt. Very bad."

"Get out of the way, old mother, or I drive right over you," the driver yelled. Behind him there were shouts and horns blared and an American officer climbed down from a jeep and started quickly forward along the line of stalled vehicles.

"A child," the woman implored. "A boy. Hurt."

The old man went to her and took her arm. She pulled away.

The driver put his head back into the ambulance and a moment later brought out his arm. In his hand he held a packet wrapped in light-brown material. He threw the packet at the woman, shouted instructions, and rolled up the window.

The old man and his wife stood on the side of the road and watched the ambulance go by. The woman felt the huge red cross brush against her like a benevolent ghost, and she made vertical and horizontal lines in the air with the hand that held the packet.

The old man stared at her. She was opening the packet. Behind him people were shouting. He took up the shafts and brought the cart to the very edge of the road. The line of refugees started past him.

The woman removed the bandages from the packet. With the bandages was a small paper packet containing a white powder. She began to peel away the bloodied cloth from the boy's wound. The blood had congealed. She pulled gently at the cloth and the boy woke briefly and moaned. She emptied the powder onto the wound and saw the pupils of his eyes roll upward and slide beneath the top lids. She covered the wound with a bandage and laid the quilt over him.

The old man watched her. Somewhere in the valley artillery thumped. Two silver jets wheeled over a distant hill from which rose columns of dense curling black smoke. The sacred land was on fire.

The old man, who could sense when living things began their slide toward death, knew the boy was dying. He thought they would be rid of him by the next sunrise. A portion of the rice would go to the boy that night. The woman would insist on it. A waste of precious food.

He walked in the line of refugees with his hands tight around the shafts of the cart, feeling in his shoulders and arms and back the mutilations in the road caused by the war machines of the foreigners. A plowing by the devils of death. The boy merely one small death amid all the other dying.

Some steps behind him the woman walked alongside the cart. Once she stopped to scoop up snow in her hands from the ditch beside the road and then rubbed the snow on the boy's fevered face. The boy woke to semi-consciousness and cried out for his mother, and the old woman felt her heart suddenly beating very quickly. A memory of cold emptiness deep as a waterless well in which only silence and darkness and demons dwelled. How swiftly the snow melted! Rivulets running across the closed eyes and alongside the slender nose and the thin small mouth. Which village is he from? Nine, ten years old. Ah, my sacred tree, caress him with your healing spirit as you did me in my childhood when I tumbled from your limb and broke a bone in my hand and the village doctor applied the poultice and I sat in your shade and you whispered to me *Arirang, Arirang, O Arirang, The pass of Arirang is long and arduous, But you will climb to the hilltop, Where the sun will always shine*, and the old doctor was astonished at how swiftly the hand healed. She scooped up snow again from the road and held the snow to the burning forehead and the boy cried out again for his mother and fell back into unconsciousness.

The line of tanks and trucks and jeeps and troops stretched ahead as far as the old man could see. Even an army of devils could not defeat so many men and machines. We return soon to the village. Before the woman finds another to share our food. Before we begin to starve.

He plodded on, pulling the cart. From time to time, when the road became steep and tortuous, the woman moved behind the cart and pushed. He sensed clearly her presence through the shafts in his hands: an old woman but still strong. Strong in everything except in the bearing of children. Permanent shame covered them. He felt again the darkness and dishonor of early-morning wakings in a childless home and he fixed his eyes upon his feet as they took the road one step at a time, one step at a time.

In the late afternoon they reached the outskirts of the city. The fields and paddies came to an end. Houses now along both sides of the road. The road littered with downed power lines and the scattered debris of broken walls.

The woman had never been to Seoul and she looked around with astonishment at the wide paved streets and the tall stone buildings. The old man had been there once before, when he had inherited the parcels of land upon the death of his father and for some reason the local town administrator sent him to Seoul and he took his papers to the office of a sneering official in a black Western suit, slicked-down hair, and pointed black shoes, who kept him waiting outside his office door for days until he realized that more money than usual would need to be exchanged for the favor of his attention. Arrogant, scornful man. Leech.

He noticed there were fewer foot soldiers and vehicles now on the main road. Damp with sweat beneath his wadded blue coat. Hands and shoulders and back trembling and aching with fatigue. Blood beating in his neck and head.

Some of the refugees were moving off the main road, vanishing into the side streets.

He heard the voice of his wife and turned to her and saw she was talking to a young woman who stood in the open doorway of a house with shattered windows and broken walls. The young woman was pointing up the road. She asked where they were from and the old woman said a village above Dongduchon. The young woman said her parents, two uncles, and grandmother lived in Dongduchon, were the Chinese anywhere near there, and the old woman said one of the sons of their village carpenter had seen Chinese soldiers in the hills just north of the village. The young woman put her hands to her mouth and hurried into the house.

The old woman turned to her husband. "We will go to the river."

"What is on the river?"

"Perhaps a doctor for the boy."

The old man looked at the boy. He lay very still beneath the quilts she had heaped on him. Cold snow, warm quilts. Where had she learned such things? Stubborn, crazy old woman. Even in old age she surprised him.

He took up the shafts of the cart and walked, following a line of refugees through the rubble of the main road. A grimy-faced little girl squatted alone on a pile of rubble, crying.

He turned to his wife, warning her with a fierce look to leave the girl alone. Here and there bodies lay along the sides of the road. Dark and fetid odors in the air: torn earth, wrecked houses, broken sewage lines, rotting flesh. Starved dogs roamed about and he thought he might catch one but he had little strength for a chase after this day of pulling the cart.

Some time later he saw through the winter twilight the dull sheen of the frozen river.

The riverbank, its mudflat skin frozen to tundra ice, slanted down in a wide brownish scraggly slope from the shell-pocked stone houses along its upper edge. A silent horde squatted upon its surface inside thrown-together shanties and near discarded oil drums in which burned scavenged wood. The flames fed upon the air through holes poked into the drums and roared upward into the darkness, casting lurid reddish dancing patterns upon the frozen surface of the river.

Beyond the opposite bank of the river was an airfield. Huge aircraft rose and landed, wing flaps extended and wheels down, like giant herons, flying directly over the old man and his wife and the boy. Earth and air trembled at the roar of their engines. Spears of light on their wings pierced the darkness.

Squatting near a blazing oil drum while the woman cooked their rice, the old man gazed at the aircraft and the burning oil drums along both riverbanks and the play of light and shadow on the river, and a memory of childhood returned to him: living men suspended head-down from chains over open firepits. A nightmare from the time when the Japanese governed the land and stories were told of their cruelties to those who resisted their rule. The flaming wood crackled, showering forth a spray of sparks. He felt on his hands and face the pulsing heat of the flames and on the back of his head the glacial air of the night. Beneath him the riverbank had softened in the heat and was oozing mud. He watched as the woman prepared their portions of rice. She squatted near the shack, cooking on the small fire she had made of wood heaped upon three stones. There would be three portions. One for the boy.

Earlier she had bartered a handful of rice for a place in a shack put up by two starving old men from the city. She had spread their pads and quilts and then had left the old man behind to guard their belongings and had taken the boy in her arms across the frozen river. The old man had squatted near the fire outside the shack, and waited.

She was gone a long time. He grew wild with hunger and began to rage within himself. Does she still not know after all these years who comes first? *First* the husband, *then* the stranger. No children from her, no loyalty from her. A curse of a woman.

Years of bitterness woke within him, working like slow poison.

Still she did not return.

After many hours the anger yielded to anxiety and fear. He could not imagine a life without her. Who would prepare food and wash clothes and work with him in the fields? Alone in old age. The curse of evil spirits.

He squatted near the burning oil drum, scanning the dark-red body of the river, and finally he saw her emerge from the shadows with the boy in her arms. His heart leaped and trembled with joy, but he said nothing.

Hours before, she had carried the boy across the frozen river, light, light as a flying squirrel. Icy air in her eyes. The boy's face beneath the shielding quilt. Will the dragon consume this one too? A double feast for his scaly belly. How he burns with fever! Another death in my arms. Where will we bury him? The first lies on the hill. His milk-name of no help: Long Life. The spirits took him to their world, leaving behind the clay of his body. But this one not yet dead. Dragon, be the dragon of courage in this one. Be the dragon that befits the jacket he wears, not the dragon of fire and death. Grandfather would fish the rivers with his net and rod, long-stemmed pipe in his mouth, straw basket on his shoulder. Why do they not fish this river? Frozen too far down? Or the river dead with poison from the war? Grandfather in the forest gathering pine brushwood for fire. No brushwood here. We will die on this riverbank. The boy will surely die. If I had a breast to give him. I am an old woman and still the spirits play with me. One son, one death. A strange boy, another death. Fire in my arms, ice beneath my feet. Play with me, pitiless spirits. An old woman. Shame, shame, you evil spirits, where is your shame? And where is the—ah, there, the shore, the riverbank. And the tent of help, where? The place of doctors and hospital medicine for our soldiers. The breathing stopped? No. Does such a fever not leave an incurable hurt? Shacks here more than on the other side. Is no one left in the villages? Our soldiers, where? The tent of doctors, where? Ah, the cross of red. What does the soldier say? No? Does he say no? Am I a cow, then, that he says no to me? Is the boy a dog? No? And the other? From the other also no? He points the weapon at me. They are here only for the soldiers? No and no? But see the boy! See the wound. He will die. Remove the fragment, seal the wound. A child. Surely. See. *Then I remove it!* Let him die here! The blood. Weak old fingers. Ah. Now. Here. See. Another death. I am a woman made for the dying of children. An earlier death punishes me. A grave wrongly placed? An ancestor poorly worshipped? But who? A long time inside the tent. They have forgotten me. Why do you still play with me, you vile and vicious spirits? I am an old woman who has been played with enough for two lifetimes. Am I outside your realm of mercy?

What? What? What does he say? He shouts. Angry! The boy.
They give him back to me. New bandage. Bleeding? No. His
fire again in my arms. Now the old one will be angry. How
he wishes him gone! Memories of the little one dead. Like this
one: light and limp and burning. Breath gone? Ear to mouth.
Not yet. Be careful—slippery. The shack, where? Ah. He
waits on the edge, his belly empty. Angry, yes. Hold him,
cover his face. This is not the jacket of a boy who works
with a plow. Silk. Special buttons. Amber? Needlewoman. A
mother? A grandmother? A yangban child? Demon dragon,
away! Seek someone else on this frozen riverbank. One is
enough. The old one wants his food. What to feed the boy? A
soup of rice and the savor of a fishtail. *Arirang, Arirang, O
Arirang, The pass is narrow. . . .*

    The old man watched as she placed the boy on the pads
and quilts and gently covered him.

    He asked, "What did they say?"

    "The army doctor would not see him."

    "So," he said after a moment. "Why were you so long,
woman?"

    "When he said it, I removed the bandage from the boy
and with my fingers pulled the splinter from his chest."

    The old man stared at her.

    "I did not know the boy had so much blood left in him."

    He shuddered with fear and anger. The demons of mad-
ness have claimed her. The boy is a curse.

    "They took him inside and I waited until they brought
him out."

    "Who brought him out?"

    "A doctor."

    "The doctor who would not tend to him?"

    "He was angry."

    The old man was silent a moment. "Will the boy live?"

    "The doctor said he will die. But there was another there

who said if he does not die it will be because of the white powder the ambulance driver gave me."

Then she had set about making their food.

Now she was feeding the boy soup made of melted snow and cooked rice and bits of fish. He was barely conscious and would not eat, but she crooned to him a song from her childhood and he ate and vomited and she cleaned him and fed him again and covered him and took up her own food and squatted by the fire, eating.

Somewhere in the fire-tinted darkness of the riverbank two men raised their voices in anger. A woman screamed. Food stolen? A fight for space?

Their supply of wood was gone. The man edged closer to the fire. He felt the warmth and emptied his mind of all thought of the woman and the boy.

The sky was black and icy with a wash of brilliant stars. Here and there along the riverbank the oil-drum fires began to die. The woman went into the shack and lay down in her clothes beside the boy beneath the quilts and the old man entered a moment later, bending down and sliding between the quilts. The boy lay between him and the woman.

The old man thought: The demons of the night will soon be walking on this riverbank. One will take the boy.

The boy lay shivering with fever. The woman sang to him softly:

> Arirang, Arirang, O Arirang,
> The times in which we live are most trying,
> To this thousand miles of river and mountains
> May peace and prosperity come.

The old man fell asleep.

Once in the night he dreamed the woman had given the

boy her breast to suckle. He woke with the quilts over his head. The woman and the boy lay silent. The air beneath the quilts was warm with the heat of the boy's fever. The old man went back to sleep.

In the morning he woke and came out of the shack and saw that some on the riverbank had frozen to death during the night. But the boy was still alive.

The woman remained with the boy while the old man went foraging for wood. The streets near the river seemed to have been picked clean and the old man wandered deep into the city. Dark-garbed scavenging shapes flitted through the rubble. Men and women wandering about dazed. Narrow side streets thick with refugees. Main roads noisy with military traffic. Was that the thunder of big guns? So close to the city? Only scraps and branches gathered so far and loaded upon the A-frame on his back. Not yet enough for a day and night of fire. If one could burn mud and stone. Perhaps break into a house? Police everywhere. Merciless. Looters they shoot.

He turned into a street crowded with refugees milling about and squatting upon the ground. A stench of dread and squalor thick in the air.

Afraid. His meager supply of gathered wood might be stolen from him if he passed through this street. He decided to return to the riverbank and soon found himself lost in narrow alleyways.

Shamed by his stupidity and fearful of attracting attention, he would not ask of others the right way but stumbled on, looking up and down the streets for the dull sheen of the river. But here the streets and alleys curved and he saw only more streets and houses and low stone walls. He wandered on and a pain began in his chest, a familiar pain, the pinpoint of pain that rose up in him whenever dread became overwhelming and he felt himself again the plaything of devils.

On one of the streets a small dog attached itself to him: tawny-skinned, ribs protruding, red tongue dangling, breath rising in brief steamy coils. He called to it and it approached warily and when he reached out a hand it shied away. He hurled a stone at it and it scampered off through an opening in a stone wall that seemed to have been sheared by a shell and lay partly in a heap of grayish rubble.

He paused, listening. The rumble of guns. He squatted down quickly near the broken wall to relieve himself and noticed jutting out from beneath a pile of stones the splintered edge of a piece of wood.

He stood and went to the stones and gazed down and then looked around. The broken wall fronted a courtyard and a stately stone house that seemed deserted. The narrow paved street was bordered by low walls and elegant homes. On the walls of some of the houses were the scars of bullets and shells. The wind made a strange high-pitched moaning sound as it moved among the homes.

The old man reached down and touched the wood and it was indeed wood and he moved away some stones and there was more wood and he moved away more of the stones and there was more wood still and he found himself after a few moments gazing down at a huge cache of shattered beams and broken boards with the nails still in them and two-by-fours and sections of wooden walls and doors. Someone's secret hoard? For barter or sale? The spirits sent me here!

He placed the A-frame on the ground and cleared away the stones and loaded the A-frame with as much wood as he thought he could carry and replaced the stones and returned the A-frame to his back and hurried away, staggering slightly beneath the load.

The street sloped and he followed it, thinking it would lead to the river, and after some while there was the dark sheen of the frozen water. He passed through the row of riveredge city houses and entered the mudflats and walked among the refugees toward the shack, conscious of the wind on his face and the hard hot looks of those squatting about staring at his find of wood.

The woman when she saw the wood said only that the boy needed the warmth if he was to stay alive and quickly set about building a fire in the oil drum.

The two old men whose shack it was lay together inside a sleeping bag and chirped merrily when they saw the wood, and one asked if they were to be included in the woman's cooking that evening.

The old man, his shoulders and back quivering from the weight of the wood and the effort of the hauling, went to the river's edge, where the frozen mud met the frozen water, and squatted there and stared across the expanse of ice at the opposite shore and its horde of men and women and children. An aircraft as large as a ship lifted itself from the earth and lumbered by overhead in a tumultuous roar of engines, then banked and slowly vanished into the pale sky. The old man watched in wonder and terror. The machines of the foreigners. How can they be defeated, these giants of pale skin, these devils on our sacred soil? Yet the guns of the Chinese are closer now. The wood I carried will warm our bodies and keep the boy alive. She will want to bring the boy. Where will we run?

The woman came over to him in the course of the day and said, "The boy may live."

"Then he can care for himself."

Her eyes sparked. "Better to have left him in the ditch."

"What are you saying, woman?"

"Will we heal him only to kill him?"

"What are you thinking?" He was angry. "Tell me!"

She said after a long moment, "This is talk about seeds that have not yet sprouted." And she went away.

In the late afternoon the wind herded dull-gray clouds over the city and snow began to fall. The woman sat near her small fire cooking their food while the two old men and the boy lay in the shack. The boy was still with fever and called out from time to time: names uttered through gasps of breath. The two old men bleated with annoyance at his cries and told the woman to silence him, they could not rest for the noise, and the woman gave them a bowl of rice and they ate greedily and were quiet.

Many died of the cold that night on the riverbank and in the morning their bodies were set out on the upper level of the mudflats, near the row of houses. The bodies were frozen into grotesque shapes, some melting into the ice so they would have to be hacked out later by those coming to bury them. But the boy, still hot with fever, remained alive.

Again the old man went out for wood. He slowed his wandering through the snow-clogged streets lest anyone sense how near the river the cache was. He walked through streets crowded with refugees and listened to talk about the war: men, women, children forced by the soldiers from the North to dig their own graves and then shot; towns and villages burned. He fled from the talk and came upon the same dog he had seen the day before but it ran from him. At the broken wall he removed the stones and loaded wood upon the A-frame and replaced the stones, and then he returned to the riverbank with the wood.

Men and women squatting on the mudflats regarded him with pinched faces. Soon they will begin to follow me. Only in the land of good spirits do such treasures go on forever.

The woman looked at the wood and said nothing: it was not for her to praise her husband for an ordinary task. The two old men, seeing the wood from their sleeping bag in the shack, squealed with joy.

The boy lay still in the pulsing circle of warmth cast by the burning wood and it was now clear to the old man that he would not die.

The following morning the woman told him that soon there would be no more food.

He squatted at the river's edge. A pitiless north wind gusted across the river. In the milk-white sky the yellow disc of the sun. Trucks rolling across the faraway bridge. Distantly the thump and thud of big guns. The Chinese like locusts in the fields. A dull heavy dread seized him. He remembered hunger, once from a time of river flood and again from a time of endless sun: firespears in his belly; locusts in his head; tremors in his arms and legs. Dark-circled vacant eyes and sunken faces and rotting gums. The long dying of his grand-mother and uncle and others in the village. All turned into shriveled foul-smelling dolls. Hunger he dreaded more than war, more than death itself. A dark and leprous scourge.

He returned to the shack and removed the small square of cloth he kept in his coat pocket and spread it on the ground. From their basket of food he took a handful of rice and placed it on the cloth, which he then tied with care and replaced in the pocket. The woman, squatting next to the sleeping boy, watched the old man in silence, no expression on her small wrinkled features. He settled the A-frame on his shoulders and, bent beneath it as if it already carried its anticipated load, he left the shack.

The snow had hardened to a slippery crust over the frozen mudflats. More refugees had entered the city in the past two days; both riverbanks were a mass of men and women. No one was fishing the river. He gazed across the river, looking for the tent with the red cross where a doctor had angrily cared for the boy. Was it near the distant bridge? Removing the splinter from the boy's chest with her fingers. All the early years docile as a cow, and then the death of the little one. A different person after his death. Holding him as he burned. First the village doctor. Then the sorceress. Helpless. Crying and burning. The boy buried on the hill and her first raging anger soon afterward at the plow that broke upon a rock in the field. The words that came from her. Much sense to wear the hat of mourning only for a mother and father: a wife is a stranger one can replace.

But the thought of her dying frightened him. How stand alone against the evil spirits?

He slipped through the row of riveredge houses and walked directly to the cache of wood.

On the narrow street before the broken wall the wind had turned the snow to ice. It blew as if through a ravine, as if across the shoulder of the hill near the village where they lived. And what of the ox in the shed? Dead by now. In the bellies of the Chinese locusts.

Near the break in the wall he took from his pocket the cloth and with care laid out the rice in a cone-shaped pile on the ice-covered earth. He gazed up and down the street, and the street, silent and deserted, put to him its mottled face. He shivered in the wind and stepped behind the broken stone wall. After placing within easy reach of his right hand a number of sharp-edged stones and a heavy piece of timber, he squatted on his haunches and waited.

He did not wait long.

The little dog entered the street from the far corner, short neck extended, nose sniffing the ground. It hesitated, shivering, and raised its head, tawny skin dull in the pale winter light. Lifting a hind leg, it pissed against the side of a house.

He watched it through the break in the wall. Reared in one of these houses? And abandoned? Nowhere to go? Waiting for its master to return? Come, little dog. Come, come. To the rice. Yes. Hunger drives one; caution abandoned. A man who is entirely a starving stomach is no longer a man. Nor is a starving animal an animal. The empty stomach runs the head and makes shit of us all. To the rice, little dog, yes, yes. Ah, yes. Now. Eat.

The dog, abruptly lifting its head from the rice, saw the old man as he rose to his feet behind the wall. It stood frozen, grains of rice on its tongue. Immediately it saw the motion of the old man's hand it began to wheel. But it could gain no momentum on the ice and its churning paws slid in all directions and it slipped and skidded. The first stone, hurled by the old man as if from a slingshot, caught it on the front right paw. Yelping, it stumbled headlong onto the ice and tried desperately to regain its balance with its remaining three legs. The second stone struck it on the back and spun it around. Its cries rang through the street. The old man was swiftly upon it but its writhing and the slippery ice made a single well-aimed blow impossible and the piece of lumber descended a number of times. He felt it in his hand each time: the thud, the thump, the breaking bones. Finally the dog lay still upon the ice, bits of rice still clinging to its limp red tongue.

The old man, breathing heavily, looked quickly around: the street was still save for the icy wind keening among the walls and houses. Much of the rice lay untouched. He spread the cloth upon the ground, gathered up the rice, laid it on the cloth, and once again tied it into a small bundle, which he returned to his pocket. He picked up the dog: warm, limp, light. All bones and air it seemed. He put it down near the pile of wood inside the courtyard, quickly loaded the A-frame, and again concealed the wood beneath stones. He paused briefly to urinate upon the stones, then placed the dog inside his jacket, its head against his neck. With its warmth upon his flesh he walked beneath the load of wood back to the riverbank.

Inside the shack he gave the dog to the woman, who took it without a word. The two old men looked at the dog and ran their tongues over their dry shrunken lips. The boy lay sleeping beneath the quilts.

The old man went down to the edge of the river and sat gazing at the wavering line where the frozen bank met the frozen water. The sky had clouded over. More snow? The ice of the river looked black. Skating on the frozen white ice of the pond outside the village. The old carpenter and his four sons. Snow-white clothes on the carpenter; many-colored garments on the children. Back and forth on the wooden skates made by the carpenter with his skilled hands. And when the youngest of the sons is suddenly too cold the carpenter lifts him and puts him inside his wadded jacket and skates with him against his flesh; and the oldest skates proudly alongside his father. Smoothly like the sailing of spirits on sunlit clouds. Smoothly like the movements of love during the three days and three nights after the wedding ceremony and the serving of the parents-in-law by the bride. Smoothly. Not like the ragged killing of the dog. Which his hand still remembered. The thump and crunch of wood and bone. Not enough time to soften the flesh. Not enough time to prepare it properly. Winter a bad season to eat dog. Glancing up, he saw the woman squatting near the shack, working over the dog. The fire leaping and dancing in the oil drum. Light snow beginning to fall: whirling flakes. Demons of cold out tonight. Ice contracting soon with a noise like thunder. More will die on this riverbank tonight. Maybe the boy too.

Guns thumped distantly. A giant four-engine aircraft suddenly overhead with outspread wings and lowered wheels, roaring over the river and landing with a reverberating blare and backthrust of engines. Like the raging Master Dragon of the Eastern Sea. But it brings soldiers. And food. What to eat afterward? No dogs on this riverbank. They know to stay away.

The snow thickened, swirling.

The woman squatted near the oil-drum fire preparing the dog. Opened, it steamed in the icy air. The air stung her small brown blood-wet fingers. Scrawny starved dog. Five mouths to feed here. The boy first. Two nights and still alive. I give a special sacrifice to the spirits if the boy lives. The promise of an old woman. A special sacrifice. One child is enough. I will think what to sacrifice. Leave this little one.

Water boiled in the kettle over the low fire on the three stones. She squatted on her haunches working expertly and ignoring the thick-falling snow.

She did not see the two men who were moving slowly along the riverbank, stopping here and there and coming to a halt near the oil drum where the woman sat.

They peered closely at the wood piled on the earth.

They were of early middle age, short and lithe, brown-skinned and raven-haired, and dressed in dark wool trousers and leather jackets and fur-lined caps and army-style boots. One carried an A-frame on his back, which he lightly slipped off and set on the ground. Without a word the two men began removing the wood.

The woman saw them and cried out.

Squatting at the river's edge, the old man heard the cry and sprang to his feet and scrambled up the mudflat to where the two men were silently piling the wood on the A-frame.

The old man asked them what they were doing.

They ignored him and continued loading the wood onto the A-frame.

The old man said it was his wood.

One of the men, without looking at him, said, "Shut your mouth, Uncle. I am not yet very angry. You don't want to make me very angry."

"You cannot take my wood," the old man said.

"Uncle, it's not your wood and we're taking it. You are fortunate that I am not yet very angry."

"I will cry thief," the old man said. "The entire riverbank will be upon you."

"Uncle, the thief here is you. But you're an old man. That's why I am not very angry."

All the time the man talked he kept loading the wood onto the A-frame.

"The wood cannot be yours," said the old man. "You steal it and hide it. Do you sell it to the rich?"

"You are now succeeding in making me angry," the man said. "It's not good for your health to do this."

"There is a very sick boy inside the shack. He will freeze to death without this wood."

"You want this wood for a sick boy? Our sacred land is filled with the sick. Consider yourself lucky I don't ask you to pay for the wood you already burned."

He helped the other man attach the A-frame to his back and get to his feet.

The woman slipped into the space before the man with the A-frame.

"You cannot take this wood," she said.

The man took a sidestep. The woman again stepped into the space before him.

The first man said, "Get out of the way."

"The boy will die."

"Blame the spirits."

"Leave us some wood."

"Can you pay?"

"We have barely enough to eat."

"Blame the North and the Chinese."

They started up the mudflat. The woman stood in the way of the man with the A-frame. The man looked at the first man, who pushed the woman roughly aside. The old man cried out in anger and stepped forward and found himself looking at a bayonet that had suddenly appeared in the hand of the first man.

"Now you have succeeded in making me very angry," the man said. He opened his mouth in a rat-toothed smile.

The old man and woman stood very still.

The man looked at them. After a moment he put the bayonet back under his coat.

"You are lucky I have respect for old people," he said. "It's one of the few things I hold from my childhood."

The two of them walked off the mudflat with the wood.

The old man and his wife stood gazing after the two men as they disappeared into the shadows amid the row of houses. Hot anger and shame brought a trembling weakness to the legs of the old man.

"There is still fire in the oil drum," the woman said. "There is some food."

They returned to the shack.

The dog was gone.

On the frozen earth were droplets of bright blood and a scattering of entrails.

They stood staring at the leaping flames in the oil drum and the simmering kettle on the small fire. Along the riverbank people lay in shacks or squatted around burning oil drums. A middle-aged woman sat motionless near a low fire outside the shack nearest them.

After a long moment the old woman said, "I will make a soup with what remains of the rice."

She squatted near the kettle.

The man stood looking at the point on the riverbank where the two men had disappeared with the wood.

He ate in silence the soup and doughy paste the woman had made with the last of the rice. A faint savor of meat tinged the soup and objects floated in it that were not rice. The woman fed the boy, who swallowed and did not vomit. The two old men ate noisily and greedily and then lay back in their sleeping bag and closed it over their heads.

Outside the shack the fire in the oil drum smoked and died away. A night of wind and snow descended upon the riverbank. Up and down the river the ice drew deeper into itself with a crunching and thundering that seemed to echo the distant banging of the artillery and the noise of the jeeps and trucks and tanks rolling across the bridge.

The old man slept and once again dreamed the woman had opened her jacket and blouse and given the boy her breast to suck. He heard distinctly the boy's drysucking sounds. He woke with a start and lay very still in a darkness so cold it seemed a ponderous weight. He could see nothing. He listened to the woman's deep slow dry breathing. But the boy lay so still the old man thought him surely dead and he raised a hand, seeking his nostrils in the darkness. With a shock of surprise he felt the boy's breath brush with warm tickling lightness against the palm of his hand. Alive! And his cheeks smooth and cool. Abruptly the boy stirred and lifted his arms and encircled the old man's neck and clung to him. "Abuji," he murmured, his cheek against the old man's face. "Abuji . . ." Then his arms slackened and fell back limply and he was again asleep.

Startled, the old man lay still and heard the loud and rapid beating of his heart. Inside his chest and shoulders and neck a fierce and urgent drumbeat. The drumbeat at the festival of ghosts. Beating, beating. The heart pounding, hammering. How is it possible no one else hears it, this thumping added to the noise of the river and the big guns and the machines and to the moaning of the icy wind?

The cold woke him. He lay with the pad and a quilt beneath him and more quilts above him but the cold wrapped itself around his flesh like a second skin. He slept fitfully and some while later woke again. Opening his eyes, he said to the coming day: Stay far from me! Shame filled him. The rough push suffered by the woman at the hands of the man. Our own people. Savages. No better than the Japanese devils. I thought he would put the bayonet into me. Shame and anger and helplessness. And his bones ached: cold and stiff as iron. Day, stay away!

For a long time he would not move. Slowly he became aware of the odd silence in the shack and he put his head outside the quilts.

The cold air struck his face and eyes. He saw through the spaces in the walls the river and the bank deep in snow and a cold gray sky. The woman, awake beneath the quilts and unable to move for the cold, looked at him helplessly. His heart turned over at her gaze and he was startled by his unfamiliar feeling of pity. Between them the boy lay asleep, breathing quietly.

He raised himself on an elbow and looked over at the sleeping bag in which lay the two old men. After some while he slid out from beneath the quilts, moved silently on hands and knees to the sleeping bag, and folded back the top.

The two old men lay very still with their eyes open to slits.

He put a hand to their nostrils. Two old men from somewhere in the city. The homes they lived in destroyed. Nowhere to go. Stay near where you live. Like the dog. Where are their families?

He felt the woman beside him. She was shivering. She helped him move the old men out from the sleeping bag. They lay face up on the frozen earth of the mudflat inside the shack.

The woman put the sleeping bag over the boy and went from the shack to tend to her needs.

The old man stripped the shoes and clothes from the two men, leaving them in their undergarments. Leave them here unburied. Better to rot aboveground than be buried in an improper grave. Bring ruin to their families. Gaunt and wasted: loose bones of men. Like the dog.

He put the clothes and shoes into the cart outside the shack and went up a distance along the riverbank to a low stone wall, where he squatted awhile in the bitter cold.

The woman was in the shack when he returned. The boy lay asleep.

"The burning is gone," she said. "The boy will live."

"If he does not freeze to death."

"You saw his jacket. Padded silk. How is it he wears such a jacket under his coat?"

"Perhaps he stole it."

"He is the son of a scholar or a yangban."

The thin arms around his neck; the smooth cheek on his face. "Abuji . . ."

"This is not a child one leaves behind," she said.

"I have no wish for this child," he said. "Do you hear me, woman?"

After a moment she said, "We must have a fire. We must eat. Others have fires. There is brush near the airport."

"Near the airport there are guards," the old man said.

The woman gazed across the river.

"I overheard," he said. "Near the airport they shoot old men and women. Even children."

She turned to him and he saw in her eyes the same look of defiance he had seen when she stood in the path of the ambulance.

Minutes later she watched without expression as he put the A-frame on his back and started across the snow-covered mudflat and the river to the airfield.

Burning? He smelled it in the dark frigid air. Wood and rubber. Flesh too? Heavy guns. The crackle of small-arms fire. Beneath his legs the river frozen to a depth of—what?—five, ten feet? If the river freezes to its very bottom, do the fish freeze too? Is the ice the grave of the fish? And do they wake with the thaw? The stream that flowed into the river where we put the goldenrod nets and caught black-and-white minnows. Flopping in the net, roasted on the pit fire along the riverbank. Taste it now: smoky and soft melting flesh. Yi Sung, tall, lost in dreams, his voice a pool of visions, telling us how as a spirit he created our village, this stone here, that tree there. Yi Sung in school in the village marketplace studying to be a scholar. Yi Sung in a Japanese jail. Yi Sung beaten with the big four-edged club. Yi Sung kicked with soldiers' boots and tortured with water. Yi Sung dead. Chinese, Japanese, Americans. Foreign devils. Burn and burn. Brushwood near the airfield. But will not burn very long. Not like the wood those two took away. Once a man who struck an old woman would be punished with death. What could I do? An old farmer. In the village when someone did wrong, there was punishment. Once he himself had been a punisher: lashing a thief on his exposed bottom in a public punishment. The one with the bayonet,

there was a look of madness in his eyes. The thought of plunging the bayonet into my flesh gave him pleasure. What is that?
Ah, the tent with the red cross. Near the bridge. The machines
come off the bridge with the wounded. So many working
there. Which one helped the boy? She pulled out the splinter.
She by herself. Grasping it with her fingers. What is happening
there near the big tent? So much running about. Machines
lining up. The wounded carried out into the machines. Brushwood near the airfield. They don't shoot if you don't come
too close to the fence. And what for food? Grass. Bark. Rats.
Look in the garbage cans near the tents. Tents being taken
down. Down?

Near the perimeter of the medical battalion, outside a
scattered line of burning oil drums that gave off the hot smoky
odors of waste fuel, he stopped and stood watching soldiers
scurrying from tent to tent, loading supplies onto jeeps and
trucks, and wounded men into ambulances. He heard orders
barked and saw vehicles pulling away. Behind him there was
a strange keening like the wind in the street where he had killed
the dog. It grew louder and he turned and saw a scurrying of
people, men and women pouring from the shacks along the
riverbank, disorder and frenzy and the lament of a thousand
voices raised in terror. On the airfield aircraft engines roared
into power, whining awhile, then gearing into full power, and
a huge aircraft rose from the ground and flew toward the east
and banked and disappeared into the clouds. Immediately two
other aircraft rose one after the other and were gone. The
bridge was crowded with jeeps and trucks and tracked vehicles,
all moving south.

He started back across the river.

Lying with the boy beneath the quilts and the sleeping bag,
the woman felt him curled warmly against her, his knees

drawn up, and heard his uneven breathing. The quilts and
sleeping bag over their heads, she saw whenever she opened
her eyes a vague whitish liquid light. The sleeping bag was
smooth and silken upon her eyes. Vague waves of sound came
to her through the quilts and the sleeping bag, sighing noises
she chose to ignore. She listened instead to the murmurings
of the boy: words she could not make out breathed through
troubled sleep. But the fever was gone: he smelled of returning
health. From time to time a trembling seized him; he lay against
her and she put her arms around his light thin frame and held
him. All bones. Like the dog. And the two dead old men. And
soon like them dead of cold and hunger if the man does not
return with brushwood and something to eat. Dead old men
unburied and rotting on the ground. No proper graves for
them, no ancestral worship, gone from the earth and from
memory forever, like an insect, a fish, a dog. Dead dog. Best
to eat in summer. Who stole? The two men and the way they
pushed an old woman. Death to them! May they be beggars!
Dragons of the mountains, consume them! And protect the
boy. A sacrifice to you if you protect the boy. A doctor to
protect and heal the boy with a poultice upon the wound. Or
a sorceress to whirl about with cymbals and drum to frighten
off the hovering devils. A scholar's son? Good fortune to have
in the village a scholar's son. Good harvest. Food. Octopus
and dried squid and eggs and batter-fried vegetables. And rice
and fowl and steamed chicken. And long life.

Light fell upon her face, and a searing cold. She opened
her eyes to a dim white world and saw above her the face of
her husband and heard beyond the flimsy walls of the shack a
tide of wailing.

She said fearfully, "What? What?"

"The Chinese!"

She rose to her elbows and swayed dizzily. He helped her
to her feet.

The boy woke and looked about with unfocused eyes and cried, "Amuni!"

The old man and woman stared at him. Ashen beneath the brown skin of his emaciated features, eyes dark and rolling with terror; drawing away from them, looking wildly around, seeing the two dead old men, shrinking back, and crying out.

The woman spoke softly, soothingly.

The boy tried to climb out of the bed of quilts, lay back in exhaustion. He tried again, fell down in a faint.

Murmuring an unbroken stream of comforting words, the woman wrapped him in a quilt. The man lifted him and carried him outside; like the dog the boy's head and arms and legs limp and flopping. He placed him in the cart and the woman covered him with quilts and the sleeping bag. Quickly they took apart the shack and put on the cart the bits and pieces of flattened waste metal.

The two old men lay in their undergarments, vacant faces turned to the winter sky. Beneath them the frozen earth had begun to melt. Muddy streamlets trickled from below their rigid heads and shoulders and stiffened legs.

The riverbank was emptying: people eddied back and forth, scurried in frantic flight across the river. Deep ruts scarred the frozen mudflats and black ice.

The old man and the woman each took one of the shafts of the cart. Pulling the cart and the boy, they started across the mudflats and the river toward the airfield and the main road.

2

They were near the outskirts of the city. Houses began to fall away; barren winter fields now on both sides of the road. Military police kept the refugees off the road, on a path between the fields and the drainage ditch. Along both sides of the road trudged foot soldiers, weary, blank-faced, heavy with defeat. Down the middle came jeeps and trucks, very fast. All were headed toward the sea.

Outside the city the road ran parallel to the barbed-wire fence of the airfield. The old man saw men and women crossing the road and climbing the embankment to the fence and tearing at the brush that grew alongside it. The woman took both shafts of the cart and the old man slipped the A-frame over his shoulders and walked along the fence, stopping to break off branches, falling behind the cart and catching up, and again falling behind.

Tank treads had kneaded the path to a rutted strip of earth. The jouncing of the cart woke the boy. Staring into the darkness of the quilts, he did not know where he was. He tried to move and found the quilts wrapped tightly around him. Pushing with both legs against the quilts, he felt reassured by their firm resistance. There seemed a rhythm to the motions of the cart and some comfort in the embrace of the quilts. He moved his arms and felt a knifepoint of pain in his chest. Frightened, he lay very still.

The woman, her legs aching, pulled steadily upon the cart. She was hurrying away from the war but the war was catching up to her. Sections of the city were burning. A choking terror lay lodged in her throat. She pulled harder upon the cart. The man fell far behind. She thought she heard him call but she did not slow her pace.

The noise of the bombardment grew louder. All around her were panicky men and women and children. In the brief pauses during the shelling she could hear their collective human noise: a kind of sustained high-pitched throbbing moan. She strained at the shafts of the cart. Away from the fiends of war. Away. Save the boy.

Inside the folds of the quilt, the boy, now fully awake, was trying to remember his name.

Days before, on the road to Seoul, angry and frightened South Korean soldiers had searched the refugees and taken away the old man's knife and ax. When he protested that he needed the tools, a soldier pointed his weapon at him and shouted that he was a North Korean infiltrator. The woman wept and pleaded. An officer intervened and ordered them on. Now, with his bare hands, the old man broke branches from the brushwood near the airfield fence and piled them on the A-frame. The fence was tall, its top section angled sharply with rows of barbed wire jutting outward. On the other side of the fence lay a moatlike ditch, and then another row of barbed wire, coiled and not as tall as the first, and the runways beyond. Planes kept taking off. Jeeps circled the perimeter of the field.

Men and women moved amid the brushwood along the road. His A-frame barely half full, the old man edged closer to the fence and was followed by others.

From the airfield came the report of a single shot.

A few of the men and women near the fence straightened and glanced briefly around. The old man thought: To die of a bullet or hunger or cold.

Two more shots were fired, then another.

The men and women near the fence gathered up their A-frames and scurried off. The old man crossed the road to the line of refugees, searching for the woman.

He walked a long time and did not see her. The airfield behind him now and the A-frame little more than half loaded, he halted again for more brushwood. He had not yet eaten that day and was trying to ignore the hunger. We will need fire wherever we sleep. Somewhere near the sea? He had never before been near water wider than a river. A boat on the sea day after day like the winged ships in the air hour after hour. What spirits keep them from sinking or falling? He saw a vision of his village: firm fields, watery paddies, contoured earth, and the hills beyond. Solid sacred graves of ancestors to the fourth generation. The village now? Surely burned to rubble and ashes. Charred homes and sheds. Broken housebeams. Floors torn up in the search for stores of food. And the ox dead and roasted and in the bellies of the Chinese and the fiends from the North.

The A-frame was full. He hoisted it on his back and began walking quickly along the line, searching for the woman.

Behind him the sounds of the war were ominously loud. Chinese fight in strange ways. Grandfather once told me. After a meal of hot rice and hot soup and kimchi and broiled fish with vegetables and pepper paste with soy. Smoking his long-stemmed pipe. Grandfather sleepy, talking through the smoke: pictures of his words in the smoke. This I saw with my own eyes in Mukden, Grandfather said. After the battle of Pyong-yang. Many many years ago. When I was a boy. Chinese cavalrymen advancing to the charge bearing fans and perfume bottles. Their servants marching behind them with Winchester rifles. The cavalrymen advancing according to proper military methods, putting on fierce faces like the god of war. Anyone seeing such faces should have fled. But the Japanese were savages, hopeless barbarians, unacquainted with Chinese ways, the wisdom of Chinese writing, the beauty of Chinese characters. The Chinese rushed upon them, breathing fire, and they did not move. It was therefore clear for all to see that the Japanese were paralyzed with fear. The Chinese general had given forth the cry of victory when suddenly a long line of Japanese rifles was raised up like a single arm, and there followed a dreadful rattle and the Chinese fell like dead trees. Grandfather's dark watery eyes through the wafting smoke of the pipe. The sweet pungent smell of the tobacco. Grandfather. How could the Chinese devils and the fiends from the North defeat the big-nosed pale-skinned giants with the blue upside-down eyes? Their bombs and machines had driven out the uncivilized Japanese who had many years before defeated the same Chinese. Is it possible? Strong one year and weak the next? The spirits play with us. A river calm one year a wild sea the next.

Where is the woman?

As far ahead as his eyes searched through the throng of refugees he could not see her.

Perhaps he had passed her, walking as he did with his eyes cautiously upon the treacherous rutted path.

But surely she would have seen him. How quickly can she be walking, pulling the cart with the boy on it? A misfortune to have stumbled upon him. A burden sent by evil spirits. Did I not offer enough to my ancestors during the last New Year's Day? Was there not wine in the cups, and chopsticks on the meat and vegetables, and spoons in the soup bowls? Did the woman and I not stand and kneel, stand and kneel, and bow low and strike our heads three times against the floor? Did not the flames of the candles flicker as the cold drafts blew across the table, indicating the spirits were present and partaking of the food? Did I not feed properly the suffering ghosts of our village, those tormented dead who wander without peace, who haunt the trees from which they fell and the river in which they drowned?

The thought that he might somehow have angered his ancestors or the ghosts of his village terrified him and left him feeling desperate and alone amid the press of fleeing refugees. What possible other hope can one have of being looked upon with kindness by the unseen powers behind the visible world, powers brutal one moment and caring the next, than devotion to the dead and belief in the unborn future grandchild? But this boy is not my child and he will not give me a grandchild and the woman has lost her mind because of this war and where is she, how can she have gone so far ahead?

He felt a sudden great need for her presence: stronger than his feeling on the riverbank waiting for her to return with the boy. It was a suffering and a dread and a yearning all at the same time. He raged at her for not being nearby; he felt himself cold with the thought that he might never see her again. Twice in these few days she has made me feel this way. That angered him even more.

He moved on, treading carefully, and feeling on his back the A-frame laden with brushwood. Still he did not see the woman.

Weak and nauseated with hunger, he paused again and scanned the distance ahead. People brushed past him, silent, scuffing the churned earth. The lines of soldiers and refugees ran now through a town of charred and battered two-story stone buildings. Power lines down and tangled. Bullet-pocked signs over abandoned looted shops. Broken doors and windows and the helpless nakedness of rooms behind shattered walls.

Immediately after the town, on both sides of the road, was a military base. Barbed-wire fences. Rows of deserted white-painted barracks. Starved dogs foraging for food, pissing on trees.

The old man thought: They permit dogs to go inside. If I enter, they will shoot me.

Beyond the military camp more fields, desolate, edged with tall winter grass. I will find something. There is always something. My ancestors will not abandon us to die of hunger. Unless this boy is an evil spirit.

Where is the woman?

He thought to retrace his steps. Perhaps he had gone past her after all. There was such a crush of people on this path.

Stay with people, the carpenter had urged them before they had all fled the village. Always remain together with others. But they had lost the carpenter during the search by military police early on the first day. Now he had lost the woman.

Then he saw her—a few yards off the road, on a barren field.

His heart beating in his throat and ears, he went to her quickly.

She stood bent over, her eyes fixed on the earth at her feet.

He wanted to say, I looked for you, woman. Why did you go so far without me? He wanted to say, You frightened me, woman, leaving me alone. Instead he said nothing.

Gray blotches stained her face. She stood unsteadily near the side of the cart.

"I am tired," he heard her say.

His heart was stirred and he felt the arousal of long-forgotten warmth. He had a vision of the two of them when young, and their three days and nights together after their marriage were about to begin, and all things were again possible: sons and abundant rains and rich earth yielding rice and grain; and oxen for the plow, so that the woman would never have to harness herself to it; and his ancestors gazing down upon them considerately from their graves on the hill beyond the village, filling their home with earthly prosperity and protecting them from harm by wandering ghosts. Yes, all things were possible. All things.

He asked her with deliberate coldness, "Where will we stay this night?"

She coughed. "I heard there are many buildings beyond the next turn in the road." She leaned against the cart, breathing shallowly. Spirit of my tree, return my breath. Father, give me your strength.

He asked, "What of the boy?"

"He woke once."

"Who is he? Where is his village?"

"I don't know. He looked at me in fear and put his head back under the quilts."

"The boy is a stone around our necks."

"If a stray dog attaches itself to you, do you send it away?"

"We should leave him, woman. What have we to do with this boy?"

She did not respond. After a moment she said, "We will not leave him to die. I am rested."

She picked up the shafts of the cart and started along the field toward the crowded path.

The old man walked beside her, too weary and ravenous to give voice to his rage. Listen to her. How does she talk to me this way? This woman, this creature, this female, this what-you-may-call-her. She who failed in her one womanly purpose: to give me sons. She gave me no one to sacrifice to my shades when I am gone. And now listen to her! He walked trembling with anger, bowed by the burden of the brushwood on the A-frame.

Beneath the quilts on the cart the boy had listened to the old man and woman talking. The sound of the old man's voice—high and gravelly—frightened him. And the words he spoke were fearful. And the dread noises of the war nearby. He had remembered his name. Now, as he felt the cart moving again, he was beginning to remember his village.

He lay still, remembering and trembling. For a long time the cart rolled across the path between the fields and the road. Then it halted and the boy, in the darkness of the quilts, heard voices raised in anger and a man ordering, "Not here! Away from here!" and a din of voices and suddenly a burst of gunfire and then screams and the cart moving quickly and after a moment the old man shouting, "Nothing but the knife for soldiers like that!" and the woman trying to quiet him.

The gunfire and the voice of the old man terrified the boy. He saw again the killing in his village and burst into tears, his teeth chattering. The wound pulsed faintly; his stomach ached; he felt the hunger in his arms and legs.

He put his head out of the quilts and the sleeping bag and saw an expanse of dull-gray twilight sky and the back of the little woman who was pulling the cart and the old man bowed beneath the laden A-frame. Who are these old people? How did I come to them?

The cold wind forced him back beneath the quilts. He lay there remembering the village and cried himself into a dark sleep.

The cart came to a halt and he woke. The pain in his chest and stomach: all the center of him hot with pain. Inside the darkness of the quilts he curled himself into a ball. Small, make myself small. Small saved me from the guns of the soldiers from the North. Small saved me from the anger of uncles after games of mischief. Small brought me into the arms of Grandmother after scoldings from the stern mouth of Father. Small, small, a bird held lightly in the hand. He fell into a dazed half-sleep. Sounds came to him as though filtered through water or high wind.

The quilt was lifted from his face. Cold air surged against him and he shivered. Opening his eyes, he gazed up at a looming shadow that peered down at him from a vast early-evening sky.

The shadow drew closer. He stifled a cry.

The shadow leaned forward and a part of itself slid beneath the boy's head and he drew back cringing and cried out. Small, very small. The dragon will disappear. Spirit of Grandfather, protect me!

He was being lifted, the quilts still around him. An odor rose to his nostrils, sour and fetid, and his stomach tightened and lurched toward his throat.

Seated now on the cart, propped against one of its sides, he opened his eyes and looked into the face of an old woman. Diminutive, brown, wrinkled; kindness shining in dark eyes set in valleys webbed and serried like earth in drought; her lips cracked, a sore in one of the corners; her nose flat; her chin pointed; her head covered with a dirty white scarf knotted in the back; in her bare hands a bowl from which rose the steam of hot food.

He grasped the bowl and heard her murmured warning, "Slowly, eat slowly," but could not heed her and gulped the soup, feeling it course down scalding inside him and his stomach momentarily recoiling—and then he remembered this woman had fed him before and he had vomited—and then he remembered she had carried him in her arms, yes, across an expanse of ice and snow to a place with a red cross—and then he remembered lying with his head upon her in snow somewhere—and then he remembered the bursts of earth as he had fled through the valley from the Chinese and the soldiers from the North and the odd thudding sensation of being struck in the chest; and stumbling along the road and the warm slippery trickling of the blood into his clothes and down his belly and between his legs.

The soup had a strange but not unpleasant flavor. Rice chaff? Pine nuts? And there seemed to be some kind of meat floating in it; he chewed it down greedily.

Another shadow appeared and stood beside the woman. This shadow too had a face, that of an old man: brown wrinkled features; dark angry eyes; wisps of graying beard on his upper lip and chin; a long-stemmed pipe held between clenched teeth. His body small, thin, wiry, even in the wadded coat. A small ugly old man, head covered by a cap with ear flaps. A large mole on his left cheek.

The boy drew back from this shadow. It had about it the dark radiance of the evil snake, the dragon, in the pond beyond his village: moist, cold, reeking, and merciless to little children fishing alone on the pond's edge. Never never fish there alone, Mother had repeatedly warned. He fished there often and had sneaked away in his special jacket from a family celebration and had been there alone fishing through a hole in the ice the day the soldiers from the North came. He slid behind the trees and lay very still and small, listening to the gunfire and the screams. He thought he saw the dragon in the water, swimming slowly back and forth, its huge form a dark shadow beneath the ice. This old man an evil dragon.

This old wrinkled angry evil dragon who had earlier in the day shouted, "Nothing but the knife for soldiers like that!" The boy handed the empty bowl to the woman and slid beneath the quilts until they covered his face and head. Small, small. If the evil dragons don't see you they go away. Good dragon, help me. Small. Like a bird in flight. Like a butterfly. Like a grain of rice. Small.

The old man had set up the pieces of scrap metal that had been their shelter on the riverbank and they slept that night in a field somewhere between the city and the sea. He woke during the night to put the last of the brushwood on the fire and saw parts of the city burning, long flames flickering red upon the low clouds. A cold wind rose from the fields and blew past him with soft moans. Scattered fires dotted the darkness, revealing dim squatting figures. He took comfort in their presence. Stay with people, the carpenter had warned. Where were they now, the carpenter and his wife and sons? Along the road vehicles moved like shadows toward the sea, only their night lights visible: the slitted eyes of evil spirits. The sounds of war distinct. What will we eat tomorrow? The boy eats for two. Suddenly stubborn as a pony, this woman. The boy will bring trouble, I feel it. Shadowy forms—starved dogs?—flitted along the perimeter of dim yellowish light cast by the flames. He called out a warning. There was a brief skittering, and silence.

His legs and back aching from the burden he had borne much of the day, he returned to the shack and slipped beneath the quilts. Between him and the woman lay the boy, breathing softly. He is nothing to me. A stranger from another village and clan. Whose son? A landowner's? A scholar's? Let them care for their own. He takes my food and my strength. How the woman clings to him. What devil pushed us into that ditch with this boy?

From the dark road came the clatter of tanks. The frozen earth trembled. After a while the old man fell asleep.

All the next morning they walked toward the sea through fields and paddies that inclined gently downward toward an increasingly wide and vacant horizon. The old man and woman pulled the cart together. Once the boy poked his head out of the quilts and saw a vast gray sky untouched by mountains and an expanse of frozen fields across which straggled masses of refugees. The immensity of the sky awed him. He smelled the brine-scented air. Incense to appease the spirits of the water? He watched the old man pulling at one of the shafts of the cart. He does not want me with them. He will send me away. Trembling, he slid back under the quilts.

Toward afternoon the woman caught a glimpse of the sea: an enormous sheet of dull-shining metal shading off into a blurred and fragile horizon. The unbounded watery expanse frightened her. Mountains and hills offered a contained and comforting world, a sense of solid place; this endless space brought dizziness and a sense of dislocation. Here the earth comes to an end. If we are not careful we will fall off into nothingness or into an underwater cavern of ghosts and demons. How will I protect the boy?

The old man too had never before seen the sea. He thought it a hundred rivers set side by side across which the spirits sent angry winds. He saw mudflats up ahead, a barren landscape descending to the sea. The scattered line of scrub brush and trees ended at the mudflats. The old man slipped the A-frame over his shoulders and went off toward a clump of brush where others were gathering wood. Taking hold of both shafts of the cart, the woman went on alone.

Later they entered a city by the sea and together with

hundreds of others encamped in early twilight near a stone jetty that extended far into the water. Putting up the sides of the shack, the old man watched as the woman carried the boy to the edge of the jetty and set him down so he could with her support relieve himself. How tenderly she held him, the quilt over his shoulders. Building a fire, he saw her talking to the boy, observed the gentle movements of her hands as she helped him urinate into the lapping waves. He felt again a rising of anger. This stranger, this stealer of food and loyalty.

The sea was murmurous in its rise and fall. Gray and dark and fringed with foaming muddy water. Waves washed across the desolate shore. The horizon, blurred by clouds and the coming evening, grew more and more indistinct, and the sea seemed to be expanding without end, while behind him the houses of the city, veiled by the dusk, were beginning to disappear. The vast and endless plain of evening. He stood at the edge of the sea and listened to the darkness and imagined the waters, driven by a sudden gusting wind, rising and washing over them all: advancing like a wall and crashing down upon them and sweeping them back out into that world of water, that engulfing emptiness. Yet so many lived here. An entire city. But deserted now. Only soldiers moving in and out of the buildings and along the bridges and roads. Earlier two South Korean soldiers had emerged from behind some trees, carrying rifles.

The old man had felt their rude hands on him. He looked away as the soldiers turned to the woman.

"What's in the cart?" one of the soldiers asked.

The woman answered quickly, "Things we took from our village. Quilts, mats, pots. And this and this and that."

"What's under the sleeping bag?"

After the briefest of hesitations, "A boy."

"What do you mean, a boy?"

"Our son," the old man heard her say.

"Pull down the sleeping bag, old mother. Very slowly."

The old man kept his head turned away.

"What's wrong with him?" the first soldier said.

"A terrible wound in the chest."

"He stinks like a shit bucket."

"Hey, Uncle, you got any money?" the second soldier asked.

The old man turned to him but did not respond.

"Hey, you hear me, Uncle? You got any money?"

"No money, no money," the old man said.

"I'll break your head if I search the cart and find money."

"No money, no food. Only this for food." He held up the tiny field animal he had found half dead in a clump of brush and saw the soldiers looking at him and then at each other, astonishment and disgust on their faces. They had motioned him forward and he and the woman dragged the cart past them and walked without a word through the darkening seaside city to the mudflats near the jetty.

Here the water was not frozen. Here it kept sighing all through the night and moving like a restless spirit back and forth across the cold wet shore.

Bursts of automatic-weapon fire woke them in the early dawn light.

The old man leaped from the quilts into a wall of freezing air and ran to the cart, ignoring the pain in his muscles and bones. The woman scooped up the boy and the quilts. All up and down the mudflats were the sounds of firing and pandemonium.

Soldiers came running across the mudflats shouting and firing their weapons into the air.

The old man started to load the metal pieces of the shack onto the cart.

A soldier ran over to him. "You get out of here now, Uncle."

The old man pointed to the partially dismantled shack, his hands making the motions of pleading.

"You move, Uncle! Move! Americans are exploding the city!"

The woman took up the shafts of the cart.

They fled across the mudflats, the pale-gray dawn sea to their right, and went along a stretch of sandy soil and then through scattered brush and more mudflats. From behind them came a low rumbling noise that grew into a heart-numbing roar and they turned and saw the entire city erupting in smoke and flame. Huge tongues of fire leaped into the air, followed by boiling clouds of dust and debris. A vast dirty brown-red cloud began forming over the city. The old man and the woman felt the ground trembling; dense waves of air struck at them and sucked breath from their lungs. The boy brought his head out from beneath the quilts and stared at the city and the old man saw upon his thin face a look of horror. Then he was emerging from the quilts and scrambling from the cart. Names and words poured from him. The old man heard "pond" and "fishing" and "dragon" and "soldiers" and "village burning." The boy ran staggering through the icy dawn, away from the destroyed city. He stumbled and fell and rose and fell again and the woman ran to him with a quilt and covered him and brought him back to the cart, murmuring to him softly, and the old man took up the shafts of the cart and walked on, the woman now alongside the cart, soothing the boy, who lay trembling beneath the quilts.

All that day they walked southward and the city could be seen burning, dusty clouds churning over it like a horde of raging spirits.

Toward evening the boy was feverish again.

Fearful, the woman put her left hand on his face and with her right hand made vertical and horizontal motions over his head. Spirit of Grandfather, protect him. Spirit of my tree, protect him.

The old man stood gazing at the boy. This burning is not from the wound. The wound is healing; its edges are sealed. Soon the woman will have to remove the threads.

From what is this burning? Perhaps from the demons of memory. They attach themselves to a person and that person wastes away. He had seen that happen before in the village. The old carpenter's brother, who lost a son one year to the flooding river: the demons of memory had eaten him to a shadow before the eyes of the entire village.

The old man found himself thinking that perhaps this time the boy would really die.

He wondered then why he wanted the boy to die. The woman would not abandon the boy. And the boy, because he was hurt and alone, would not leave on his own. But he would certainly leave later to return to his village. What if his village no longer existed? Then he would return to his family and clan. But what if all were destroyed, as had happened to so many? Then they would give him over to the government or to an orphanage. But what if the woman refused and the boy chose not to leave? Still, why should he want the boy to die? A helpless child.

The old man then found himself gazing at something within him that he had never before seen. All knew of the unseen world beyond the everyday realm of appearances; but he had never thought there might be such a world inside himself: unexplored and cavernous. And because he could neither understand nor name it, he could not see which spirit or demon lurked within it, and that was for him the greatest fear and bewilderment of all.

Still, he was certain he wanted the boy to die.

❖

They slept on the ground near a stand of shattered trees. Dead branches littered the shell-pocked earth but soldiers had come earlier among the refugees and warned against making fires. The woman could not sleep for the cold. All around were footsteps and moans and the sibilant whispers of the spirits of the trees. She lay beneath the quilts and sleeping bag alongside the boy and heard clearly the talking of the trees: the anger of spirits not properly fed, the vengeance they planned—this one's child would drown in a pond; another would burn of fever; a third would topple headlong from her swing . . . Up and down on the swing, the warm spring wind on her face; higher and higher, until her bare feet sent the peach blossoms raining down upon her, and higher still, to the very heaven above. White anemones glistened on the slopes of the hills and frogs had begun to bring their music to the nearby streams. Up and down and higher still, embraced by the kind spirit of the tree. The boy lay beside her, very still . . . Mother came running that day with news of my marriage: our names and birth days were in accord; men would soon arrive from the bridegroom with gifts of cotton and silk and fine shoes. The boy lay rigid and strangely still. Perhaps he will die after all. What do the spirits care about how many children they take from one mother? Did they not take three from the wife of the old carpenter? Up and down and higher and higher a terror this creature beside me and where will I run they are all dead their hands tied behind them in their shallow grave and why is she singing, this old woman. She felt the boy suddenly stirring, was stabbed by his moan. Raising her stiff arms, she felt upon her face the dry coarse flesh and broken nails of her hands, then drew across the underside of the quilt the vertical and horizontal signs taught her by her mother and murmured soothing words to the boy. The old man slept on, breathing deeply. Stiffening, the boy cried out. Hands tied behind their backs and earth on their faces. Grandfather and Mother and Father and and and earth in their open mouths and eyes and their heads in odd positions as if without bones and and and running. Who are these two old people and demons of fire on my eyes and what is this old woman doing now singing. Mother would sing with earth in her mouth and there are fiends in these broken trees I hear them and they will kill the boy this night. But she swung on the swing higher and higher and when she could go no farther, at the very height of the arc, at that instant of hesitation between up and down, she leaped from the swing toward the trunk of the nearest shattered tree, arms and legs swimming through the air, and entered deep into the core of the tree, and in the depths of the tree she encountered the clammy foul-smelling spirit, clung to it, sank her fingers into its hooded eyes, heard its piercing scream, felt its tail lash her legs and grasp her thighs. A stone-shaped cry stuck in her throat. *The pain!* She clutched the scaly throat, pressing upon it all her weight, and the creature, writhing, released its grip and slithered from her with tiny moans of defeat and vanished into the heart and root of the tree; and the old woman lay very still, a heavy throbbing in her chest and thigh. She mounted the swing and flew up and higher and took with her the pain of the boy to the blossoms on the boughs and to the heaven beyond. She slept then in a delirium of hunger and dread and through the occasional bursts of automatic-weapon fire that stitched the distant fringes of the refugee camp.

The old man heard movement, a moan of pain. A burst of light, iridescent sparks rising. The lights were inside his eyes. He thought he must be dying. Death welcome. But to be buried in this desolation. Or not to be buried at all.

That last thought brought him sharply awake. His lids scraped across swollen eyes.

He saw the woman with her head over the boy's exposed chest. She had brought her mouth down upon the boy and was gnawing on one of the black stitches.

The boy gave out a little scream and pushed with his sticklike arms against the woman's head. She moved her head slightly away and with her fingers tugged at the stitch, which she then pulled through the puckered skin of the healed wound.

The boy watched in horror.

The scar, about two inches in length and parallel to the right collarbone, was red and ugly. Again and again she put her mouth to the wound and each time chewed at length, making dry grinding noises with her teeth. The boy felt her wet lips and tongue upon his chest, smelled her breath. She drew the stitches through and held them dangling in her fingers, black writhing strings, and threw them clear of the quilts.

She was done. Her mouth ached. She tasted the blood from the broken gums around her teeth. Covering the boy's chest, she murmured to him soothingly; and the boy lay still.

The old man looked at them in the dawn light that filtered through the partially open top of the sleeping bag and knew the boy would not die of the wound though they would probably all die of the hunger that would soon finally and firmly settle upon their lives.

Many already lay dead on the beach. They lay where they had died in their sleep and no one moved them after the removal of their shoes and clothes. The woman, trembling with weakness, shook the vermin from the quilts and sleeping bag. The bugs scattered on the sand; the lice she would attack again later.

Carrying the quilts to the cart, she suddenly grunted and bent over, and stumbled off behind some trees.

The boy stood a moment, glancing around, shivering.

The old man felt the boy's eyes upon him. He helped the boy into the cart and wrapped him in quilts.

Knowing now the boy would not die of the wound, the old man thought to study him closely and saw, in the folds of the quilts, a frightened trembling creature with dark hair, a furrowed brow, dark soft eyes arched with fear, a slender nose, the center of the mouth bow-shaped and then dropping to thin pale lips, a soft rounded chin, high-boned cheeks, and a long thin neck. His lips were parched and cracked. There were reddish sores on his face.

The old man looked away from the boy, shivering with uncomprehending anger at the spirits that had sent him to them. Why did they return his life to him? Is he strong with magic?

"Are you able to speak?"

Hesitantly the boy nodded. He means to hurt me.

"What is your name?"

"Kim Sin Gyu."

"Where are you from?"

The boy named a place north of the old man's village, a slight breathlessness in his high thin voice.

"What is your father?"

"My father?" A lengthy pause as the boy looked away and then looked back. "A scholar. A poet."

"Where are your people?"

This time the boy did not respond.

"What happened to your people?"

Still the boy said nothing.

"You have no one?"

"I had a dog."

The old man looked startled.

"A dog with three colors. Badooki was his name, because of his spots. Three Four I called him sometimes, a bad name, to tease him. Three colors, four legs." The boy paused a moment, his eyes swollen with memory. "Badooki ran away when the noise began and and I was afraid to run after him because I thought they would see me and he ran across the pond into the forest and and and . . ."

The boy stopped. His breath came tremulously from the exertion of speaking.

There was a pause.

The old man looked intently at the boy. "Tell me again your name."

"Kim Sin Gyu."

"How old are you?"

"I am eleven years old."

"What do you want us to do with you?"

The boy was quiet. He saw clearly the malice in the old man's dark eyes and was frightened and bewildered.

"You do not belong to us," the old man said.

The boy began to cry.

The old man looked away.

From the direction of the hills in the east came a flurry of rifle fire. The old man saw the woman hurrying toward them. Her face greenish, drained of life. Others had begun scurrying from the beach. The old man and woman took up the shafts of the cart.

The sea, driven by winds, foamed upon the shore. The old man and woman, together with others, walked with their backs to the sea toward a region of ice-covered mountains.

In the early afternoon they reached a small valley. The noise of the war came only faintly there.

With what remained of his waning strength the old man gathered wood and lit a fire. The woman prepared a soup of melted snow and winter grass and the remains of a frozen jackdaw she had found earlier on the beach. Wild dogs circled in the darkness just beyond the light of the fire. The boy sat up and ate, holding the bowl tightly in his shaking hands. His eyes kept darting about and he would not look directly at the old man. The woman watched him eating and spoke silently to the tree of her childhood and to the spirits of her father and grandfather.

The next morning they continued south along cart paths, away from the fading sounds of the war.

During the early hours of the day they came to a narrow valley and the boy was able to walk awhile, leaning on the side of the cart. The woman, overjoyed, refrained from speaking lest she cause him undue fatigue. The old man was glad they did not have to drag the cart with the boy in it along the stony floor of the valley. Tall steep walls of boulder-strewn granite rose on both sides of the valley, darkening it with spectral shadows. The wind blew a wall of stiff cold air through the valley and soon the boy could no longer walk and the woman helped him into the cart and covered him with the quilts and sleeping bag.

"Hungry," he pleaded.

"Soon."

"Hungry," he said again.

She turned away and took up the second shaft and walked alongside the old man.

"How far?" she asked.

"We will stay with the others."

"There are some who are not continuing."

"They will not live long."

"The boy needs to eat."

"The boy. The boy."

"I cannot go on."

"When we stop I will make a fire, catch a rabbit."

She knew he had no strength to hunt rabbits. "I am ill and will never again see our village."

"Stop!" he ordered her, glancing fearfully around. "When the spirits hear such talk they know immediately where to go."

"I am an old woman and with me they have known a long time where to go."

"If they come to you they will notice me."

"Are you afraid? How many times have you told me you are not afraid?"

"They will notice the boy."

That silenced her.

"Climb into the cart," the old man said.

"Ah, no." She was ashamed.

"Climb in, woman."

"I will not."

"What can I do for the boy if you are ill?"

She considered that and a moment later climbed in. The old man pulled the cart along the narrow path through the valley.

She lay shivering next to the boy. The pain in her stomach frightened her. She trembled violently and felt the boy move close against her, giving her of his warmth. He drew the top of the sleeping bag over their heads and they lay in the darkness.

The war was now far behind them and they could no longer hear it.

In the evening the old man made a fire and tried to cook a soup of snow and grass. There was a taste in it of earth and stone. The woman could not eat and sat bent over outside the rim of firelight, vomiting. The old man sat in the heat of the fire. The boy squatted on the other side of the fire, away from the man, and listened to the sounds the woman made. What will I do if the woman dies and the man sends me away?

But the woman did not die. In the morning she walked

on trembling legs alongside the cart and in the afternoon they reached a broad plain and the man, gathering brushwood, stumbled upon a small rabbit, which the woman skinned and roasted that night. The three of them sat around the fire, eating.

Hundreds were scattered throughout the plain in the frozen night. There were fires all through the plain and no sound of the war. No one seemed to know with certainty where they were going. It was rumored there was a huge refugee camp with food and warm tents somewhere beyond the next range of hills.

In the morning the old man was sick with cramps and fever. He pulled the cart together with the woman until his arms and legs grew numb. They were on a cart path in a narrow valley. Caves pocked the sides of the hills.

The old man lay in the cart, pulled by the woman and the boy. I will die here in this cart behind this woman I no longer know and this boy who is a stranger. This cart will be my deathbed and this valley my grave. For this all the offerings to the spirits. For this all the festivals to the ancestors. For this all the gifts to the ghosts.

After a while the woman and the boy could no longer pull the cart with the old man. They stood alongside the cart, bent and trembling with exhaustion. Then they dragged the cart to the side of the path and squatted beside it.

All the rest of the day refugees flowed past them without stopping. So many. The woman had not thought the war had undone so many. Each with eyes fixed upon the ground. Men beneath A-frames. Women with children strapped to their backs and bundles on their heads. Sighs, moans, a cry from a child. Carts, wagons, a few oxen. No one spoke to the woman or the boy. The old man raised his head from time to time and watched them going by.

The air was clear and bitter cold. The sky, a deep icy blue, faded slowly into evening.

The old man was barely conscious when the last of the refugees straggled past. Stars began to appear. A partial moon glided across the jagged tops of distant mountains. By its ghostly light the old man saw the shadowy figures of the woman and the boy as they stood alongside the cart looking at him.

BOOK
TWO

3

Slowly, by the light of the climbing moon, the woman and the boy dragged the cart with the old man still on it across a length of craggy ground to the nearest cave.

Fearful, they stood at the mouth of the cave staring into a darkness that would not open itself to their eyes. The dank fungus smell of sun-starved stones and earth brushed against their faces and filled their nostrils.

Perhaps spirits live here, the woman thought. Will we disturb them?

The boy had never before seen a cave. Its dark gaping mouth, a little wider than the cart and a few inches taller than the woman and set at the base of the towering granite wall, frightened him.

They left the cart just inside the mouth of the cave, where it was sheltered from the tundra wind blowing across the valley, promising snow.

The woman went behind a clump of bushes by the side of the cave to relieve herself. Then she called softly to the boy and the two of them gathered winter grass and brushwood and she lit a fire directly outside the mouth of the cave. She boiled snow into which she placed various kinds of winter grass and weeds. She offered the soup to the spirits of the cave. Then she turned to the boy.

"Do not eat the grass," she reminded him. "Drink only the soup."

The boy stared ravenously into the bowl but did as she ordered.

She went to the cart and gently pulled down the top of the sleeping bag from the face of the old man. She was startled by the fever heat that rose from him. He stirred and moaned. His eyes glimmered darkly in the light of the fire. "Drink slowly," she told him, but he could not keep down the food and after a while she left him and returned to the fire.

She took some fresh brambles and lit their ends in the fire. Holding them over her head like a torch, she went past the cart into the cave. The boy came and stood beside her.

The cave was about twelve feet deep, its granite walls black, fissured, craggy. Its curved ceiling rose from its mouth to a height of about ten feet at the far wall. A layer of frozen moisture covered the walls with a black glistening sheen. The floor of the cave was of hard clay. Over its center, where they now stood, hovered the noxious stench of stagnant pools and pestilential marshes. At the foot of the far wall was another opening, about the height of the boy and twice his width. When the woman saw the second cave she began to tremble. Cave leading to cave to the very bowels of the world. Surely spirits live here. What will happen to us?

She led the boy back to the mouth of the cave and tossed the burning brambles into the fire. She spread pads and quilts on the earth alongside the cart and motioned to the boy, who lay down beneath the quilts.

The old man moaned loudly and called to her from the cart. She helped him down from the cart—how hot his gaunt flesh was!—and held him as he squatted near the brush outside the cave and turned her head away as foul-smelling waste poured from him. She led him back to the cart and piled quilts on him and he lay helpless and shivering.

If he dies I will be left alone with the boy and we may both die. If he lives he will send the boy away.

She felt pressing upon her all the vast mountain above the cave: a world freighted with cold malevolence. Squatting close to the fire, she gazed at the faces that appeared to her in the leaping flames. Father would smoke his pipe staring into the flames. The children never permitted to go near him when he sat that way. Especially the girls. Smoke in his narrow eyes and wispy beard. How he disliked the girls. A weight upon him, a dark shame. Five girls, one boy, from the first wife. After the fifth girl a second wife and three boys. Then my sisters sold off to an arranger of marriages, a fat perfumed lady in billowing skirts who came and went with a servant in a curtain of hushed voices. Outrageous to sell them! Mother would not let him sell me. *Stubborn woman!* he shouted at her. But I was not sold. Dancing leaping vaulting flames: faces of the dead.

The boy lay beneath the quilts listening to the hot crackling of the flames. The same noises: the flame-sounds of wooden walls and grass roofs burning. The very air on fire. Mother, he thought he heard himself cry out, there was earth in your mouth. And Father looked strange with his head bent back that way. Grandfather, if the old man dies the woman will not send me away. But can we survive without the old man? Will I die in this cave with these strangers? And what of your wish that I become a scholar and a poet? The fire crackled loudly as the woman placed more brushwood on the flames. Burning wood and straw and the ox bellowing in the shed and the pigs squealing and the frenzied dogs running back and forth and Badooki vanishing into the forest and the air swollen with reddish smoke.

The woman rose from her place by the fire and slipped beneath the quilts beside the boy. He smelled on her the smoke and heat of the flames, and cringed. The wound in his chest had begun to throb again.

Outside the cave the moon was long gone and the fire began to die. Creatures edged toward the cave but did not enter. The wind blew through the starlit darkness and before dawn brought with it a fall of thick dry snow that quickly covered the valley.

In the early morning the snow ended and the wind died away. A platoon of South Korean infantry entered the valley from the south. The soldiers approached the cave in which lay the old man and the woman and the boy but did not stop to look inside. They passed on through the valley toward the destroyed city on the sea, leaving behind their tracks in the snow.

The woman thought: How silent the boy is. A sealed room. Mouth always tight, eyes always averted. Slender hands. Like the hands of one of my sisters bought by the fat arranger of marriages. Soft delicate movements of his shoulders and neck. A dancer. Is there a girl inside this boy? His penis and testicles are well formed, no question there. He will not speak unless spoken to first. Often when he is alone he inclines his head as if listening for something. He is a carrier of too much memory. His eyes are like the big mirrors in the marketplace: I see in them his burning village. What is happening to me in this madness of war? Can a stranger's child be so quickly loved by an old woman? Are the spirits playing with me? Have they nothing better to do than torture again an old woman already scarred by their previous attentions? Turn away from me, spirits. Leave me in peace. How many more years have I? Will each year be a time for your sporting? Is my life a playing field for your games and laughter? Why have you sent me this boy? He said to me earlier in answer to my question, I am eleven years old, and I said, I am told your father and grandfather were scholars, and he said with pride coloring his face, Great scholars and famous poets to ten generations, famous in the North and in the lands of the Chinese and known to emperors and kings, writers of poetry and lovers of Chinese characters and teachers to the sons of ambassadors and landowners, and Grandfather and Great-Grandfather once in the service of the government in Seoul. I said, Tell me if you wish what happened to your mother, and he said, tears in his eyes, My mother has earth in her mouth and sings when she sews or prepares the most delicate of foods, my mother tells tales of tigers and birds and swinging contests, my mother lies in the burning village in a grave so shallow it was not even to her ears but earth was in her mouth, I saw it after they left and all around the air was on fire and and there was a rain of burning ash and I ran into the forest but could not find Badooki Three Four and I ran through the forest and into the valley and and and. . . . Calm yourself, calm yourself, I said to the boy. The old man tells me you are called Kim Sin Gyu. We were many generations in our village, the boy said with great agitation. Why did they burn it? We were like the rocks of the earth, the hills of the valley, generation upon generation to the time of the Chosen dynasty and perhaps earlier. Grandfather told me. How do they come like a raging river, like a swarm of locusts, like an army of madmen, and kill us and burn us so that not one not one not one remains and if I had not earlier disobeyed my mother, if I had not gone to the pond to watch the fish gliding in their winter sleep beneath the ice, if I had not gone with my dog Badooki whom I sometimes tease with the name Three Four to the pond near the forest outside the village, I would have earth in my mouth and be in that shallow grave because they killed all the children too the friends of my age and even younger and spared only the babies they left the babies crying on the ground amid the flames. How he trembled as he spoke! His fingers scraping at the sores on his face and I took hold of his hands to restrain

him because he was making the sores bleed and he cried and
then was still and I heard strange sounds inside the cave
which I tried desperately to ignore. The spirits stirring in
their sleep? I thought the boy had fallen asleep but after a
moment he said, Don't I know how the man feels about me?
What have I done that he should hate me even before I have
spoken a word? I know he will send me away or give me
over to an orphanage. And he cried and I said, Calm yourself,
calm yourself, you know nothing of this yet, it has not happened therefore how can you know it, the man is not the
only one here with you, there is a woman here too, who
cared for you when you were with the piece of metal in your
flesh and helped to heal you and will not so quickly let you
be abandoned or given over to strangers, calm yourself or
you will again be ill. He grew silent and I said after a long
moment, If you wish, only if you wish, you may call me
Mother. And he said, No, with respect, you are not you are
not my mother, how may I call you Amuni?

The boy woke and remembered his name and where he was.
Raising his head and looking about, he felt immediately the
pulsing in his chest and chose to disregard it. The wound has
healed. How can what has healed become not healed?

He then realized that the woman was not beside him and,
feeling a flutter of alarm, rose from the quilts.

The cave was bright with sunlight reflected off the snow.
On the cart lay the old man, asleep, his face reddish brown
from the fever, his lips and eyelids quivering. The boy saw the
black craggy walls of the cave and the opening at the far end
and the small furry winged creatures clinging to the ceiling
and the walls. He shivered at the sight of them and hurried
from the cave.

Where was the woman?

Snow covered the valley and the mountains; a hushed landscape of gleaming white beneath a morning sun in a brilliant blue sky. The valley, about half a mile in width, ran in length for about three miles until it reached the far range of mountains. With a shock the boy noticed the tracks less than thirty feet from the mouth of the cave. Then he saw other tracks. A dog has been here too. Where is the old woman?

Nearby sounds startled him and he jumped back into the cave and poked his head out cautiously and saw the woman emerge from behind a clump of tall brush, the A-frame on her back half laden with brushwood. He rushed forward to help her and felt again the odd throbbing of the healed wound in his chest.

They piled the brushwood near the firepit she had dug the night before outside the mouth of the cave. He asked, "Who made the tracks in the snow?"

"Soldiers. Can't you see? Those are tracks made not by rubber shoes but by boots."

"And a dog was here too."

"Do not let wild dogs come near you."

"What are those things on the walls inside the cave?"

"You must not go near them. They are the spirits of the cave."

The boy shivered. After a moment he asked, "Will the man live or die?"

She said impassively, "He will die."

The boy glanced at the cart and then lowered his eyes.

"There is a small stream on the other side of that clump of brush," the woman said. "Between the brush and that line of boulders. But it is entirely frozen and there are no fish in it. Even the banks are frozen."

"What will we eat?" the boy asked.

"There will be something. Under a rock or in the earth. I will find something." And she set about making a fire.

She put water on to boil and was gone awhile from the cave and returned with things in her closed hands and made a soup of some kind and afterward she and the boy worked a long time gathering brushwood and piling it in front of the cave, leaving enough space between the brushwood and the cave for the firepit but effectively concealing its mouth. Then the woman tried again to feed the old man but he could not keep down the food. She squatted by the fire with a quilt over her shoulders staring into the flames and listening to the soft moans that came to her from the cart.

The boy wandered off in the direction of the stream and found it a few yards beyond the mouth of the cave: a narrow cleft of solidly frozen water that ran from a line of tall boulders at the base of the mountain wall and disappeared into an impenetrable clump of thornbushes. Here the morning sun was concealed by an outcropping on the mountain across the valley and though the wind had died the boy shivered in the shadowy air.

He approached the mountain wall and found he could slip through the crevice that lay between two of the boulders. Prickly frozen snow covered their surfaces and scratched his hands. Almost to the other side, he bumped his chest and gasped at the stab of pain that ran through him from the point of the wound. He placed a finger over the tear on his jacket and gently pressed down and felt the pain in his neck and head and deep into his chest. It is almost like the first day of the wound. How can that be? Then he forgot the wound, because he had found the point where the stream entered the valley: an ice-covered pool like a small pond at the very base of the mountain wall, not more than a hundred feet from the mouth of the cave.

He looked around carefully and waited, listening. Was

that the beating of his heart or was there in the distance the thunder of war? No, it was his heart drumming and thundering in his ears and causing the strange pulsing of the wound. He shivered and approached the edge of the pond and squatted beside it and looked down at its surface of ice that glinted white in the shadow of the mountain. With trembling hands he cleared the snow from an area near the edge of the pond and found a large sharp-edged stone. He held the stone in both hands and stepped carefully onto the ice, which held firm.

He moved cautiously to the center of the pond, where he squatted and began to chip at the ice with the stone.

Thicker than he had thought at first; it took a while to break through.

The coldness of the water stung his fingers and sent a shock through him. His teeth chattered. He could see the pale gelid flow beneath the ice: half-frozen liquid like a thick gray-green soup through which moved sluggishly a nearly dormant six-inch-long silvery fish.

He chipped at the edges, widening the hole. All the time he worked he felt the throbbing of the wound.

Near the pond was a clump of brush. He broke off a long thickish branch and, hacking at it with the stone, managed to split one end, which he then separated into two prongs for the length of about three inches. This he took to the edge of the hole, where he squatted and waited.

A thin silvery fish slid slowly into view, carried more by the tiny eddies of the pond than by its own motions, and the boy speared it deftly and left it beside him flopping about on the ice and then quickly speared two more. He picked up the fish and, holding them still alive in his hands, turned to start back to the cave and found himself facing three dogs.

They stood between him and the boulders. Two large dogs and one small one. Long-nosed, brown-haired, red-tongued, hungry.

The boy, more startled than frightened, remained very still. The dogs did not move. He could hear their short rapid breathing. After a moment he scraped snow from the ground with his shoes and found some small stones which he tossed at them. They dodged the stones agilely but did not move from the boulders.

The boy held one of the fish over his head and one of the big dogs barked and started toward him. The boy threw the fish as far as he could, feeling as he did a tearing pain in his chest, and the dogs scampered after it. He made his way between the boulders and returned to the cave.

He gave the remaining two fish to the woman, who took them from him without a word. She put snow into a pot and brought it to a boil. She did not clean the fish but put them whole into the boiling water.

The boy squatted by the fire and thought of the small dog on the other side of the boulders. He is not like my Badooki; he has only one color. But he is the same size. Is the spirit of Grandfather speaking to me through that little dog?

The woman let the soup cook a long time and then she and the boy ate it as a hot jelly. But the old man would not eat.

In the late afternoon the woman said matter-of-factly to the boy as she squatted in the mouth of the cave, "We will wait until he dies and then we will cover him with stones in the cave."

The boy said, "But the dogs."

The woman said after a moment, "The spirits of the cave will care for him."

"And what will happen to us?"

"We will go through the valley and the mountains and try to find the camp for refugees."

The boy raised his eyes and looked out at the narrow valley. "And if there is a snowstorm on the way?"

"The spirits of our ancestors will not abandon us."

The boy squatted in the mouth of the cave watching the sun disappear behind the mountains and deep shadows gliding across the valley floor. Then he looked in the direction of the stream and there was the smallest of the three dogs standing near the dense growth of thornbush and gazing at him, red tongue hanging from its mouth, tail slowly wagging. A small lean brown part-shepherd dog. The boy could not see the other two dogs. Perhaps they cannot come between the boulders. Am I thinner than those dogs? Only the little one can get through?

The fire had burned down to a bed of reddish-gray ash. The boy looked into the pot. About an inch of the jellied soup remained in it: what the old man would not eat.

Squatting near the mouth of the cave, the old woman watched without a word as the boy took the pot and left it about ten feet in front of the dog and returned to the cave.

The dog approached cautiously, backed away, came forward again, warily sniffed the pot, buried its nose in it, withdrew a few feet, looked around, loped back to the pot, and, knocking it over on its side, swiftly devoured its contents. Then it barked twice and turned and ran toward the boulders and disappeared.

The boy cleaned the pot with snow and returned it to the firepit.

Before dark he went back to the pond and caught four fish. The three dogs were there again and the two large ones scampered after the fish he threw them. The little one remained behind and he tossed it a fish, which it deftly caught in its mouth and began immediately to devour.

The boy gave the two remaining fish to the woman, who buried them deep in the snow outside the mouth of the cave and in the morning once again cooked them to a hot jelly which she and the boy ate. She held up the head of the old man and tried to force the food into him but he spat it up and moaned. His eyes were red and dry with the fever. She melted snow in a separate pot and some of that he drank.

"He will die tomorrow or the day after," she said later to the boy as they squatted near the fire. "How strange. I thought the spirits would take me first."

The boy responded with an odd choking sound.

The woman turned to look at him.

"My head," he murmured.

"What?"

"Hurts."

"Where?"

He began to raise a hand, and stopped. His face was strangely flushed. The woman saw him fall slowly sideways from his squatting position, pupils rolling into his upper lids and only the whites of his eyes showing. He lay near the fire in a dead faint.

Trembling, she washed his face with water from the pot. He is burning with fever. From what? The boy opened his eyes and moaned.

"Head," he whimpered. "Head."

She carried him to the place in the cave where the quilts lay. As she spread the quilts over him she brushed against his chest and he stiffened and cried out. Gently she opened his torn coat and wadded jacket and shirt and undershirt and searched for the wound.

She saw it with a shock. Under the right clavicle. Red and puckered and jagged. A foul sickly-sweet odor rising from it. Red streaks radiating from the lips of the wound, and parts of the wound whitish gray and crusty. She pressed gently with her fingers along the ridge of the wound: gray-white gelid fluid spurted through, a thin jet nearly striking her face.

She looked in horror at the wound and put her hand on the boy's chest. It seemed on fire.

She covered the boy and bathed his face again. He moaned and talked incoherently of the pond near his village turning into a river and Badooki lost in the forest and becoming a small red bird and his grandfather lying in a field of grass gazing through his spectacles at a flying gray mouse-shaped furry spirit. She put more brushwood on the fire and squatted near the flames, a quilt over her shoulders.

She thought: Now both will certainly die and this cave will be their grave. And I will die here too, but for me there will be no stones. The man wanted me to send the boy away and now they will lie here together. Somewhere there is great laughter among the spirits.

She felt too weary to be angry. She did not know what to do.

All that night she kept the fire burning and bathed alternately the faces of the boy and the old man. If there are spirits of kindness left anywhere in this war let them find this cave. Let them find these mountains and this valley and this old woman who makes a promise of many offerings to any spirits who find this cave and heal the boy and the man. These words she said to herself again and again. On occasion as she moved back and forth from the fire to the boy and the man, murmuring the words aloud, there came from deep inside the cave the flutter of wings and the tiny movements of small hairy forms.

At dawn she left the cave and found the space between the boulders and barely managed to edge her way through. Between the boulders and the base of the mountain the air seemed colder than it did near the cave. The surface of the hole in the pond had iced over during the night and she chipped at it, using the stone left there by the boy. With his wooden tool she caught five fish. When she rose wearily to her feet she found herself besieged by the three dogs.

The boy had told her of the dogs.

She walked slowly toward them, speaking softly, and when one of them growled she raised one of the fish high and let them see it and then tossed it far away. The two large dogs barked and raced off after it but the little one remained in its place. She tossed it a fish, which it caught and began to eat. Then she returned to the cave.

She was trying to feed the boy when she heard a noise from the mouth of the cave and looked up and saw the little dog as a silhouette in the morning light. The boy, semi-conscious, saw the dog too and called out strange words the woman did not understand. She poured some of the soup into a small pot and left it at the mouth of the cave and the dog ate quickly and then sat on its haunches watching the woman. When the woman went to put more brushwood on the fire the dog ambled over to the boy and sniffed him. She watched the dog sniffing the boy's head and chest, its tail wagging. It barked once and the sound went ringing through the cave and there was a brief fluttering of wings and then silence. The dog lay down next to the boy outside the quilts. The woman sat by the fire exhausted and fell asleep.

When she woke the dog was still on the floor of the cave, its long nose nuzzled against the boy's chest. She looked at the dog and shivered. Something. Some dim memory.

The man moaned. She helped him from the cart and supported him as he squatted outside. The sun shone bright on the snow. She gazed out at the mountains and the valley. No people. No soldiers. Where was the war? Had she and the man and the boy wandered from the earth into a world of spirits? If we are in a world of spirits they will either kill us all or help us all. Or are the spirits fighting among themselves over us? Do those who wish to help us need our help to succeed?

The man groaned. He could not walk without her help. There was little left of him but bones. She brought him into the cave and helped him onto the cart. If there are spirits who need help, how can I help them?

She remembered then once in her childhood watching the village sorceress tend to a neighbor, an old woman. This memory surprised her, because she could not recall ever having thought it before, and with a tremor of fear she found herself thinking it had been sent to her now by a spirit.

She took clay from the floor of the cave and put it into a pot and heated it dry and with a round stone ground it into a fine powder. She poured hot water over it and brought it to the old man and tried feeding it to him. He would not take it but this time she poured it into his mouth and held him as he choked and gagged, and some of it he spat out and some of it he kept down.

She then went to the boy and bathed his face and lifted his jacket and shirt to look again at the wound. The stench from it made her gag. But the dog, who had slunk away when the woman had come over to the boy, now reappeared and the woman smelled its heat and watched in surprise as it put its mouth to the boy's chest and sent its smooth wet red tongue darting forward in a few brief tentative licks at the wound.

The boy suddenly opened his eyes and moaned and pushed at the dog's head. The dog retreated but a moment later was back and its red tongue licked hungrily at the suppurating wound.

The boy lay very still, his eyes partially open and only the whites showing.

The woman looked at the jagged hot cleansed wound and covered the boy and spoke softly to the dog, who lay down beside the boy.

She squatted by the fire, dozing and dreaming. In one of her dreams she was sailing high into the air on her swing and then suddenly falling and a dog licked at her bleeding leg. She woke. It seemed to her she had been asleep only minutes but the sun was almost to the western mountains. She rose and ground clay and fed it in a soup to the man and then uncovered the boy's wound, which was oozing pus again, and watched as the dog licked it clean. She went to the pond and brought back three more fish, after feeding one to the two dogs. A second she threw to the small dog and with the remaining two she made another soup. Then she bathed the man's face and fed him hot water and clay, and bathed the boy and fed him hot jellied soup, and once again let the dog cleanse the wound.

She slept that night on one side of the boy and the dog slept on the other side, on the floor beside the quilts, and all through her sleep it seemed to her she heard the sighs and flutters of the spirits of the cave.

The next day she did the same things she had done the day before; and again the following day.

On the morning of the fourth day she looked at the boy's wound and saw the swelling was gone and it was clean. The boy lay cool and deep in sleep, the dog beside him. The man sat up in the cart and weakly demanded food. She fed him the jellied soup and afterward he lay back and slept. She thought fearfully: This is a place filled with the power of healing spirits. I will walk carefully and be silent.

In the afternoon she returned to the pond and after feeding the two dogs brought back three fish, one of which she gave to the little dog. She cooked a soup and offered it to the spirits of the cave and after a while fed it to the man and the boy and then ate of it herself.

The fevers were gone from both the old man and the boy but both were skeletal and could barely stand without the help of the woman. The boy lay on the ground beneath the quilts and hugged the dog to himself in his sleep and the man lay on the cart staring at the valley and trying to remember how he had got to the cave.

"From where are the fish?" he asked the woman.

She told him. He glanced in surprise at the boy.

"And the dog?"

She told him that too.

"We cannot live in this cave forever," he said.

"First get back your strength."

"We need meat," he said.

She did not respond.

"We need meat, woman," he repeated.

She got up and walked out of the cave. He stared at her and lay back and closed his eyes.

The next morning two jet fighters flew over the valley and the boom of their supersonic speed reverberated through the mountains and stirred the creatures on the walls of the cave. They went fluttering and chittering through the air. The dog scampered off and the old man and the woman and the boy left the cave and sat in the sunlight.

After a while the woman got to her feet. "I will bring back some fish."

"We need meat," the old man said angrily.

She went off toward the boulders.

The old man sat with his face in the sunlight. He had not thought he would ever see sunlight again. The woman could not have done this without the boy. How strange the way the dog healed the boy's wound. Once I heard something like that. A dog licked to health a sword wound that would not heal. In the time of the Japanese. The carpenter told me that story.

The boy opened his eyes and, squinting in the sunlight, saw the old man looking at him. His heart raced and he turned quickly away. How he dislikes me. I see it. Why? The old man fidgeted with annoyance. There is something about this boy something and yet see how he helped the woman and knew to catch the fish and brought in the dog. Ah, my arms and legs. The sickness has made me into water I can hardly move I am like the woman after she bore the child and could not move and the wetnurse had to take him. We fed her light seaweed cooked in water and sesame oil, I remember. And later I bought some meat at great cost to feed her and bring her to her feet. See how the boy sits looking into the sun. His skin so thin I can see through it to his pulsing blood. Blue veins along his cheeks and on the side of his head. Smooth delicate papery skin. The son of scholars and poets. And landowners too, no doubt. The rich. No surprise the fiends from the North killed them all. They drink our blood, the landowners. But what does the boy know of such matters? He is a child. Still. Scholars and poets, and in the service of kings and emperors. If we are overtaken by those fiends from the North and they find us with this boy they will kill us all.

He heard a noise and saw the woman returning, her arms loaded with brushwood. She lay the brushwood down with care a few feet from the mouth of the cave.

"Is there fish?" the old man asked.

She shook her head and put snow into the pot and put the pot on the fire. Then she went back to the load of brushwood near the mouth of the cave and the boy saw her lift out of the wood the limp body of the little dog. She squatted over the dog with her back to the old man and the boy.

After a while the boy looked away from the woman and stared across the white valley at the afternoon sky.

The old man watched the woman and listened to the silence. This is a world filled with spirits. Is this boy, then, a child of spirits, that he saves my life again and again? Is there good magic in this boy?

The woman made a soup and offered it to the spirits of the cave. Then she set it before the old man and the boy. The old man saw the meat in the soup and had some trouble holding it down. The boy ate slowly and silently. When they were done the woman ate. Spirit of Mother, she kept saying to herself. Spirit of Grandfather.

They slept together that night on the earth of the cave, beneath the quilts and the sleeping bag, the boy between the old man and the woman.

The next day the boy felt strong enough to return to the pond, where he speared four fish. When he started back to the boulders, with the living fish in his hands, he saw the two large dogs blocking his way.

He spoke softly to the dogs. They stood very still, watching him. An offering, he murmured, to the spirit of life. Grandfather taught me that. An offering of thanks. He placed two of the fish in front of the dogs and returned to the cave.

The woman lay awake part of that night and listened to the fluttering among the spirits of the cave. There seemed a restlessness to their movements. Furry wings beat the air, bodies hurtled through the darkness. They are telling us we have been here long enough. Even spirits of kindness grow impatient with men. Also there is danger in becoming too familiar with spirits. And what more can the boy do for us here?

Two days later, on a cold gray morning, they left the cave.

As they went along the valley the war returned to them. On occasion they came upon the remains of bodies alongside the cart path. At one point they stumbled upon a graveyard of rusted jeeps and tanks where a battle had once been fought. They were journeying south, deeper into the valley, and thought to take the path through the mountains and go in search of the refugee camp. A bitter north wind scoured the valley. They took turns at the shafts of the cart.

4

For a time in the afternoon the old man and the boy pulled together on the shafts of the cart and the woman pushed from behind. Icy winds, dense and crystalline, scratched their eyes. The sun lit up the summits of the mountains and sharply angled rays ran across the steep ridges, breaking the valley into a fierce pattern of light and dark. They were warmed by the sun as they walked in it and chilled by the shadows. Walking in the sunlight and treading upon his shadow, the boy saw on the snow in front of him the prints of boots and rubber shoes. Others had passed through this part of the valley and packed down the snow on the cart path. When? In the nights?

As they approached the foothills, the walls of the valley grew taller and steeper, the valley narrower. Firs and pines, branches bowed with snow and ice, covered the juncture of the valley and its hills, and at one point a narrow line of larch advanced determinedly up the slope of a low mountain and yielded only to the granite face and thinning air. Along some of the foothills the trees seemed to be climbing perpendicular walls, and the ridges and towers leaned inward over the valley like, like what? like, the old man suddenly remembered, like, yes, the barbed-wire top of the fence near the airfield outside Seoul where while we were gathering brushwood—when?

how long ago?—while we were gathering brushwood they
fired their weapons at us and a man standing not twenty feet
from me was struck in the chest and spun quickly around and
tumbled face forward into the brush and those of us near him
scrambled to gather up the wood he had loaded on his back
and run and they fired at us again but no one was hit; the
peaks leaned inward over the valley until they formed a nearly
enclosed bower; and to the woman, pushing the cart from
behind and wondering how long its wheels would last, to the
woman the distant sliver of sky, pale blue and too soon emptied
of the sun, mirrored the narrowing of the valley floor and cart
path into a pebble-strewn fissure: a ravine at the very root of
the world.

    Blue-gray shadows entered the valley. Walking alongside
the boy, the old man thought: Where is this place? What is it
called? In the North I hunted one winter in a valley like this
with my uncle and two cousins. A deep narrow river running
through it and the trees down to the banks. How old was I?
Fourteen? Fifteen? Long before the war between the Americans
and the Japanese. Uncle shot six pheasants. And two huge
boars. We came upon them burrowing for acorns in the snow.
Coal black, big as bears, large tusks. One of them, wounded,
charged to within nine feet of me and Uncle. Smelled him and
saw his yellow eyes. Uncle gave me a piece of his liver in the
hut later. Raw and warm and dripping. Cousins took a long
time to stalk and shoot a goral. Uncle said I should become a
hunter, not a farmer. Stay with me, I'll teach you to hunt. You
take the rich Japanese and Russians out hunting. From far off
we saw leopards and even a tiger. But Uncle would never kill
a tiger. A sacred animal, the tiger. Uncle said tigers protected
the wild and miraculous ginseng roots. A single drink prepared
from the ginseng root and a person will never shiver in the
cold or suffer in the heat, Uncle said. You grow strong and

immune to all illness. You live until you are eighty or ninety. But it must be the wild red ginseng root, Uncle said, not the cultivated one. What is this valley? Where are we? Have I fallen into a dream of my childhood? Thoughts caused by not enough meat? Wise to have held the raw liver of the dog until this time. Keeps fresh in the cold. Warm it just a little near the fire. Eat it tonight warm and raw. One piece for the boy. What shall I do with this boy? Is he good magic? Let him return with us to our village? But he is not of our blood.

The old man sensed a change in the direction of the wind and felt the floor of the valley begin to climb. A faint keening accompanied the wind here, like the sound on the street in the city where he had slain the little dog. He trudged on, his shoulder muscles sore and quivering. Legs treading cautiously the icy pebbled path. Sweaty with exertion beneath the heavy cap and wadded clothes. Five days ago nearly dead, and now, see, still alive. Where will we sleep tonight? Maybe a cave somewhere. They took away the pieces of the shack, those soldiers. Our soldiers. A knife to them!

Entering the foothills, he saw propped up against a low boulder the badly decomposed body of a woman. Stringy black hair; empty eye sockets. She had been left in her clothes but her shoes were gone and the soles of her feet were torn to black-and-red strips from the pebbles and the ridged razorlike ice and her legs had turned black. Black too her sticklike arms and hollow face and the stubbly remnant of her nose.

The woman saw the body and looked away. She murmured words taught her by her mother and quickly made horizontal and vertical motions with her right arm. It might be me in that cave if not for the healing spirits. Animals have been at her. No peace for her spirit. All the thousands and thousands of spirits of those slain in this war. No rest. No one to bring them offerings. Terribly lonely. As my spirit would have been had the boy and the man died. But better unburied than to lie in a wrong grave.

The boy stared a long moment at the dead woman and turned away. Mother with her eyes wide open and frozen. Nose firm and straight and blackened with dirt. Earth in her gaping mouth. Maybe the fire did not destroy everything and I ran away too soon. Maybe I'll stay with them in the refugee camp and return with them to their village and then go back to my village to see if anything remains. Maybe someone is alive and and Badooki returned and is waiting for me and and I should go back and and and. . .

The woman left her place at the rear of the cart and went to the front and took the place of the old man, who then slipped the A-frame over his shoulders and walked off toward the trees to gather pine brushwood.

From somewhere came the sudden chop of a helicopter echoing through the hills and advancing toward the valley. Snow fell from trees and small stones cascaded down a steep gully. But the sounds and echoes faded and the whispers of the wind returned and now there were stars in the twilight sky.

The woman and the boy walked on, pulling at the shafts of the cart, and the old man, working among the trees, loaded brushwood onto his A-frame and never let the cart slip for too long out of his line of vision.

Before dark they halted at a ledge carved out of the base of the mountain wall and the woman built a fire. An overhang extended nearly the length of the ledge. The old man, helped by the boy, turned the cart on its side and angled it against the mountain. The cart and the mountain gave them two walls, with the fire as the third. On a flat rock next to the cart the old man placed tenderly the small box that contained the spirit of his father.

The woman filled a pot with snow and boiled it and put into it the small black mountain snake the man had found curled in sleep beneath a rock during the day. She offered the food to the spirits of the mountains, thinking, Are the spirits of these mountains like the healing spirits of the cave, and they had the soup and then ate the raw liver.

All that day since leaving the cave in the valley the old man and the woman and the boy had not exchanged a word.

"I have not thanked you," the old man said now to the boy when the soup and the meat were gone. "I want to thank you."

The boy bowed his head. The woman smiled joyously to herself.

"You are a clever boy. Who taught you to fish?"

"Grandfather."

"The scholar?"

"No. The father of my mother. He had long poles and high boots and fished in great rivers."

"What did he do, this grandfather?"

"He owned many farms."

"A farmer?"

"No. He owned the land."

"Ah."

"He was also a great hunter."

"Ah, yes?"

"But I never went hunting with him."

"Ah."

"Have you ever gone hunting?"

"When I was a boy. But my memory of it is dim."

"My mother's father said I should go hunting and not read all the time, but my father and his father would not permit it."

The woman listened and remained silent.

"When we come to the camp," the boy said, "will you send me away?"

The man shook his head and scratched the mole on his cheek. "If the authorities ask, I will say you are not my son. But I won't send you away."

"Will they take me away if I am not your son?"

"I don't know that."

"What must I do not to be taken away?"

"I don't know the law."

"There was nothing left when I ran from the village. It was on fire and everyone was dead. Otherwise I would not have run away."

The woman turned to look at the boy.

"I ran up and down and through the village to find someone. I did not run away because of cowardice."

"I never said that."

"I was very frightened, but I am not a coward. I even tried to put out the fires. The air was on fire."

"I have never even thought it," the old man said. "But you are not of our blood."

"And you will not send me away?"

"I won't send you away until we know it will be good for you."

"Can I return with you to your village?"

The old man shook his head. "It is not your village and I am not your father and this woman is not your mother. Now we must go to sleep or fatigue will make us sick again."

Quickly the woman unfolded the mats and quilts and sleeping bag and shook them out. She spread them upon the ledge, directly below the overhang. The wind as it moved through the ravine brought to them the cries and hooting sounds of night animals. Curls of smoke and heat from the fire blew across the ledge.

The boy had gone off to the side beyond the ledge to tend to his needs.

"Listen," the woman said quietly to the old man, "you would let this boy go?"

"What are you asking?"

"This is a boy with strange power." She knew how he thought.

"What do you mean, woman?" He trembled.

"The pond. The fish. The dog."

"Yes?"

"There is magic in this boy."

"Magic?"

"He may be helpful to us."

"Let him take his magic and go home," the old man said.

"I saw how the dog came to him. How it cured him."

"We are too old for a young boy. He brings with him memories."

"What memories?"

"The life I might have had. All the children and grandchildren stolen from me."

"And from me," the woman said after a moment.

"In the camp we will find a place for him. Let him take his magic. I have no need for magic."

"Speak softly," she cautioned. "There are spirits everywhere."

He cringed and looked fearfully around.

The boy returned and knew from their sidelong glances that they had been talking about him.

"We will die in this cold if we do not keep up the fire," the old man said. "The woman and I will take turns."

"I will take a turn," the boy said.

"You're a child," said the woman.

"I'm a boy. And the wound is healed."

"It is too cold for you to be awake now."

"I will take my turn," the boy insisted.

"Speak to him," the woman said to the old man.

"If he wants a turn he should have a turn," the old man said, thinking of the additional sleep and the fewer hours of numbing torpor by the fire.

"But he is a child," the woman said.

"He is more than a child," the old man said. "By your own words."

The woman began to respond but thought better of it and was quiet.

"Make sure you don't fall asleep by the fire," the old man warned the boy. "Or it will be the last sleep for us all."

"When shall I wake you?"

"Let the fire burn down to this height"—the old man stooped and marked the air with his hands—"and then add wood to it to this height. After you have put wood on it a fifth time, wake me. Good night, Kim Sin Gyu."

"I do not know how you are called," the boy said.

"Call him Father," the old woman heard herself answer to her own astonishment.

"Woman!" said the old man in anger.

"How may I call him Father?" asked the boy, his voice suddenly rising. "How?" He was crying. "How how how?" He wiped at the tears and looked fiercely at the old man. "I will call you Uncle."

The two old people were quiet.

"Good night, Uncle," the boy said. And to the woman he said softly, "Good night."

He turned his back to them and put a quilt around his shoulders and squatted by the fire.

After a moment the woman slipped into the quilts on the floor of the ledge. She thought: This boy will live all his life with those memories. He is too much inside his village.

The old man slid in quickly beside her and she felt the tautness in his bony frame. He scratched himself furiously and shivered and ground his teeth. Slowly he settled into sleep.

The boy squatted on the ledge, tending the fire.

He sat cocooned inside the quilt with only his eyes showing. The fire offered a dancing nimbus of light and caressing fingers of smoke and heat as it played across the ledge and over the two figures sleeping beneath the quilts. Minutes passed and from the mountains came the piercing noises of a night creature: three long shrill cries ringing through the darkness. He shuddered as the sounds penetrated him and brought a tingling to the back of his neck and the tips of his fingers and toes. What had made those fearful noises? A bird caught in its nest by an owl? A rabbit foraging outside its den and suddenly snapped up by a leopard? Are there leopards here? Flames dancing in the wind with a whoof and a puff and streams of sparks whirling off into the terrible darkness. Mother told me once a story when I was a child a fish a rabbit a turtle. Warm voice of Mother with cold earth in it now. A rabbit a turtle a fish. The queen of fishes. How she snapped at a worm one day and caught a hook through her mouth. Pain! With a burst of energy she broke the line and escaped with the hook still in her mouth. She became very ill from the evil hook. Pain and fever. All the scholars of her kingdom were summoned to her palace. Grandfather listening to the story smoking his long-stemmed pipe and smiling behind the smoke. Father studying a book of Chinese characters but listening too behind his studying. The turtle, fat and scheming, announced that only a medicine made from the liver of a rabbit would heal the queen. I am acquainted with a rabbit, I see him walking now and then along the beach, I will bring him to the palace of Your Majesty. In fact the turtle did not know the rabbit very well but hoped that his cunning would help him make a great reputation for himself with the queen . . . Has the fire burned so low already? Did I fall asleep? We will all die of the cold if I fall asleep. More wood. Build it to here, the old man said. This mountain wind like a wall of ice. Remember how I put my hand in snow once to show off to my friends how long I could keep it there and when I took it out I could not feel the fingers, they were of a strange color, and the village doctor clicked his tongue and said two more minutes and I would have lost some of the fingers and Father was dark with anger. This is a foolish boy, he said. I have under my roof a foolish boy . . . Well, what did the fat and cunning turtle do? It dragged itself up to the beach and luckily there was the rabbit, who looked surprised and asked the turtle why he was out of the water. For the view, said the turtle. We have better views than this, said the rabbit. Ah, you should see the view in the water, said the turtle. Mountains, forests, valleys, caves, and great open plains. And most especially the palace of the queen . . . More wood again? How quickly it burns down. Quietly, so as not to wake them. Animals in the darkness, I hear them. Hungry dogs? A leopard? Or are there leopards only in the North? . . . I would like to see the palace of the queen, said the rabbit. Hop on my back, then, urged the turtle. And the rabbit hopped onto the back of the turtle and down they went into the water and the rabbit was delighted by the view of the undersea mountains and valleys and caves and plains. And the royal palace was splendid and the rabbit was brought to the chambers of the queen, where he met the scholars and the doctors and was offered warm rice wine and a delicious omelet with soybeans, millet, maize, and rice with vegetable leaves. As the rabbit sat eating he overheard two servants talking about the need to obtain his liver to save the life of their queen. This frightened the rabbit but he kept his wits and when summoned before the queen again the fire is down so quickly is this the third or fourth time the third time it must be I see shadows moving beyond the flames night animals put on more wood but remember only as high as the old man said the rabbit put on a calm face and said he would be delighted to give his liver to save the queen but the liver could be put in and taken out it is worn like spectacles and he had left it on the beach so as not to get it wet and he would be happy to bring it to Her Majesty. Do go and fetch it, said the doctors and the scholars. And the rabbit climbed onto the back of the turtle who returned him to the beach where the rabbit informed the turtle that he had only one liver and he intended to keep it and off he went leaving the fat scheming turtle to answer to the queen for his foolishness. And Grandfather chuckled with the pipe in his mouth and and Father smiled with his eyes on the Chinese book and Mother murmured good night and Badooki barked somewhere outside and and and the fire is down again and this quilt is not warm enough against the cold and if it were not for this fire we would all be frozen and dead by now like that woman and Mother with earth in her mouth. Foolish turtle and wise rabbit. Be wise like that rabbit, Grandfather said to me the next day. And Father said, He does foolish things, he daydreams all day by the pond, and Mother said, But he is only a boy. Now all with their hands tied and their heads in queer positions and earth on their faces and in their mouths. He dozed briefly and woke in terror and did not know for a moment where he was and then he saw the fire was too low and the wind dead and the air searing with arctic stillness and he put more brushwood on the fire, its prickles stabbing his hands, and he dragged himself over to the quilts to wake the old man.

At first he would not waken and the boy shook him. Then he opened his eyes and gave out a cry of alarm and gazed frenziedly about him.

Startled, the boy took a step back and almost fell over the quilt in which he was wrapped.

"You told me to wake you." He heard the quivering in his voice.

The old man stared at the boy as if he did not know him. "What is this? What is this?" His eyes looked wild, his voice was hoarse and phlegmy. He coughed and cleared his throat and blinked fiercely.

"It is the fifth time," said the boy, trembling. But is it the fifth time? Did I fall asleep and count wrong?

"What? Ah. The fifth time."

The old man climbed unsteadily out of the quilts, grunting, scratching himself, adjusting his clothes.

The boy slipped the quilt from his shoulders and handed it quickly to the old man and in the instant before he disappeared into the quilts on the floor of the ledge felt the shock of the cold air penetrate his clothes to his skin: a dousing with ice water. Shivering uncontrollably, he curled himself against the woman. Small. Very small. The rabbit in its den. The little dog sleeping next to me in the cave. Tiny white spot on its brown nose. Wagging tale. The spirit of Badooki in that little dog? Small.

The old man sat in the heat thrown off by the burning brushwood watching the flames and the smoke rising into the darkness. I was dreaming I lay dead with cold earth heavy upon me and the boy reached in and pulled me from my grave. This is a boy with good magic yes but Uncle once said, Magic good or bad you stay away from it, too much good magic or too much bad magic both bring you harm in the end. Be a hunter and the spirits won't know you're alive and will pay no attention to you good spirits or bad spirits. Listen to me, my nephew, too much good and the bad spirits become envious. Be a hunter and live in a village in the mountains of the North or the East look there look at your cousins good sons and healthy boys they will be fine hunters one day how patiently they stalked this goral look at the size of its antlers and the color of its skin. Or be a farmer with your father in the South but stay far away from this or that magic and remember it is written, The world is a seething torrent, what man can guide it? Is it not better to choose a master who flees the world than a master who flees from this man or that man? You see, hunting is my master and together we flee the world and live among these mountains and the animals know me and even those I kill I live with their spirits and bring them offerings and so far they have not harmed me. The old man shivered, engulfed by this torrent of words forgotten for nearly a lifetime. Memory is a grave best left undisturbed. Why remember now? The boy. His presence returns to me buried memories. What sort of magic is that? Let him go back to his own village. Ah, the fire has burned low. I will let the woman sleep and take her turn for her. She has done enough these days. Tending to the boy and to her husband in this war. The world is a seething torrent. Uncle quoted from the words of the wise Master. He should thank his spirits he did not live to see this war but died instead happy in his mountains. I do not need these memories. This boy, there is something about him, he will drive us crazy with his presence. Again the fire low? Does this wood burn too quickly or is the remembering taking so much time? The air so frigid like when I was a boy plunging my arm to the elbow in winter into the river near the village and feeling the water jellied with cold. He will call me Uncle. I don't need him to call me Uncle. I have no one to call me Uncle. I was my father's only son and I am near the end of my life and with me everything dies.

A faint stir rose to his ears, a vague rustling of the air in the mountains all around.

He looked up in fear.

A thin wash of light had slipped imperceptibly across the eastern sky. Animals stirred. The tops of mountains and trees were returning to view.

He shook his head, dazed. How did the hours pass so quickly? Is the boy a sorcerer with power over memory and time?

He threw more brushwood onto the fire and sat tense and fearful in the quilt, watching the flames roar upward to meet the day.

Later, alone, he struggled to raise the cart, ignoring the stiffness in his muscles and bones, and the boy heard through the quilts and sleeping bag the noises of the scraping wood and came out of the warmth and helped him set the cart on its splintered wheels. He watched as the old man lifted the box of his father's spirit from the flat rock and held it tenderly, murmuring to it, and then placed it on the cart.

The woman put her head out of the quilts to the light of morning and looked around, squinting in astonishment. Then she stared fiercely at the old man, who shrugged and turned away.

"You did enough in the cave," he muttered.

"What is enough?" she began to ask but could not yet find her voice. She cleared her throat and spat and said again loudly, "What is enough? What do you mean?"

"The time passed. There was no need to wake you."

"I am your wife," she said bluntly.

"Then help us prepare to leave this place."

The boy stood by, listening.

"I am not so old yet that you need to spare me," she said.

"Woman, a few days ago you said the spirits would soon take you."

"A few days ago the spirits had already carried you off. We snatched you back. If you can stay up with the fire so can your wife."

"I hear you," he said.

"If the boy can stay up with the fire so can your wife."

"Woman, you are a roaring in my ears." Stubborn noisy creature.

Her bones hurt but she felt fully awake for the first time in days and she gazed clear-eyed at the mountains and the cart and the boy, who stood nearby with his eyes cast down.

"The sleep was good," she said. "I thank you for the sleep. Now we will go."

The man thought: She does not know her place anymore. Where does it come from, this bossiness, this belligerence? I treat her with kindness and she is angry. Is it because of the boy? What is he doing to her, this carrier of magic, this sorcerer?

"I don't know where this refugee camp is," he said, taking up one of the shafts of the cart. "If it is more than a day's journey—" He left the words unfinished. Work your good magic, sorcerer, and find the refugee camp. We may not survive another night in these mountains.

The path, barely wide enough at times for the cart, climbed slowly and wound through the mountains and soon it was above the tree line and the sun glinted on the ice faces and snow gullies and the wind cut like swords. All morning they followed the path through the mountains and encountered no one. Yet others had been through here; there were tracks in the crusted snow.

The old man and the woman pulled on the shafts of the

cart and the boy pushed from behind. They rested three times before the sun reached its zenith: the old man or the woman raised an arm and released the shaft and they huddled in quilts near the cart to warm themselves, their vaporous breaths on each other. Nothing was spoken during those times. During the third time, as they squatted near the cart beneath the blankets, the boy noticed the splintering in the wheel. The rim was chipped and cracked and the body of the wheel—all of it wood, from rim to mortise holes, solid wood with no spaces—had begun to work loose from the hub. He sat shivering inside the quilt between the old man and the woman and stared at the wheel. I won't tell them. The old man has probably already seen it. There are no tools anyway, how can we repair it? Maybe it will last until the refugee camp.

Pushing against the cart later, the boy tried to raise the wagon slightly off the path each time he thought the loose wheel would encounter a large stone or ridged patch of ice. He did the same still later, when he took the shaft and the woman went behind to push. The old man sensed the break in the rhythm of the pulling and during the next rest the boy saw him looking at the loose wheel and noted the glance the old man gave him. After the rest the old man took the shaft on the side of the bad wheel and the boy, on the second shaft, raised the cart together with him to spare both wheels on rough patches of path.

The woman, near exhaustion, noticed none of this. She realized the man was not foraging for brushwood. No fire would keep them alive in these mountains this coming night. Here were no protective caves, no ledges, no tarns, but steep ridges, bouldered ravines, spiky towers, deep snowfields. The man wanted them to travel as far and as fast as they could and so would not relinquish his place at the shaft of the cart to go off for firewood now. She looked around dazedly. What am I saying, there is no wood here, only stone and ice and snow. But why are there no people? Where did they all go, all who passed us the day the man took sick? Vanished into the mountains? Did we take a wrong turn somewhere? But there were no turns off this path. Did we miss a turn because it lay buried in snow? But we would have seen tracks.

She went on pushing the cart and talking to herself, dazed and bewildered. Why do they keep lifting the cart? Do they think the cart will fly? See how they raise it and put it down. What are they doing? They have turned this into a game. This pleased her, the thought that the boy and the man had somehow conspired to make the hauling of the cart into some kind of a game. But it was not long before she noticed with a shock of dread the loose wheel and from then on she too tried to ease the burden of both wheels upon the path by lifting the cart together with the boy and the old man, but after some time she gave it up, she was close to collapse.

In the late afternoon the path abruptly leveled and began a long gradual turn, a steep drop on one side and a nearly perpendicular headwall on the other. They witnessed a cascade of snow down an avalanche gully, heard the distant rumbling. They witnessed too the descent of shadows like the curling of smoke entering the mountains and the coming twilight and the first of the stars. Strange how the stars canopied all the sky and shone cold and blue and orange and hot: an enormous expanse of sky as if stars had fallen and earth and sky were now a single horizonless starry heaven. Mountain air affects the eyes, Uncle said, and the heart and lungs, you see the whole world in a different way. And now so we found the boy and came all this way only to die here in these mountains what kind of spirits are you to do such a thing to an old woman there is no strength left in me even for anger but if there were how I would hate you. And if I had not run away if I had stayed maybe someone would have been alive and and I could have lived with them but no one was alive and Badooki had also run away and and I would have died in those flames everything was burning the houses the air the bodies and and and look all the stars everywhere stars the ice on the mountains reflecting the stars in the sky and in the snow stars and stars.

The old man brought the cart to a sudden halt, causing the woman to bump her head against the back. Stung sharply by the blow, she felt herself lifted out of her darkness. The boy let go his shaft and stood trembling with fatigue, unable to move.

The old man stood at the edge of the road, staring off into the darkness below. "Fires," he said hoarsely.

The woman and the boy stared into a distant abyss in which tiny flames flickered and minute figures moved about.

Now they pulled and pushed the cart, not caring for the wheels, and soon they had to lean into the cart and hold it back for the steep descent of the path.

Near the end of their descent, the air almost black with night, the cart path briefly paralleled and then joined a wide level dirt road along which a ragged line of refugees advanced slowly toward a vast plain dotted with shanties and firepits and burning oil drums. Trucks went by on the road, heading north, only night lights showing. At the far end of the plain lay a military compound encircled by a concertina-wire fence lit by oil drums and patrolled by armed guards.

The old man and the woman and the boy followed the road as it left the mountains and entered the plain.

5

U p ahead soldiers stood warming themselves near drums of burning oil at the checkpoint where the road branched off into the plain. Orange flames lit their faces and glinted off the white letters on their helmets. The air was thick with the hot acrid stench of the smoking fires.

As the old man and the woman and the boy approached the checkpoint a soldier called out to them in Korean and the old man and the woman quickly put down the shafts of the cart. The boy came out from behind the cart and slipped between them. He felt the woman's fingers grip his arm.

The old man looked fearfully at the soldier. Short, thin, a hooded fur-lined combat parka and gloves. Closed, arrogant face, the face of magistrates and bureaucrats, the face of landowners. A rifle slung over his shoulder; a weapon on his hip. He looks at us knowing our lives are in his hands. Search again? His fingers on my arms and back and chest and crotch and legs. And again search the woman? The boy so frightened I feel him trembling. What will I say if they ask about him? Do not lie to our soldiers, the old carpenter warned us, they shoot anyone suspicious, they think soldiers from the North conceal themselves among the refugees from the South.

Squinting into the firelit darkness, the old man took a rasping breath of cold air and felt a sudden bubbling and surfacing of recent memory. On the road from Seoul, beyond the airfield: jammed with infantry and vehicles. Looking for the woman. The line of refugees along the narrow path between the road and the frozen fields. A man suddenly bolting from the path and starting at a run across the road. Slipping through the line of infantry and dodging between two jeeps, running with a load of brushwood on his back. A single rifle shot, a ringing sound, and he stumbled to his knees and fell on his face. Like a straw sack of grain. Two soldiers dragged him to the side of the road and threw him into the drainage ditch. Why did he run? Suddenly possessed by a demon? A man of middle age, dead face-up in the ditch, his chest a spreading mass of blood, men and women fighting over his wood. I forgot it and remember now. Where do they go when they vanish, memories, and what brings them back? The boy is afraid. I see his eyes. Be rid of him now and not have him as a weight anymore. But the woman will be angry. Stubborn woman. He is talking to me, what is he saying?

"You, Uncle, you."

The soldier, his flashlight in the old man's eyes, was a voice only, his face and form gone in the blinding light.

The old man blinked and squinted.

"Your papers, Uncle."

"Ah, we have no papers. We left all our papers in our house in our village. Ran very fast from the Chinese and the soldiers from the North."

The woman closed her eyes a moment. A wave of fearsome memories: the young son of the carpenter running through the village shouting, Chinese in the hills! and the panicky scramble for the cart and throwing into it the quilts and pads and some pots and bowls and food and the box with the spirit of the man's father and fleeing through the paddies to the main road along footpaths barely wide enough for the cart. Certainly the ox dead now and the village ashes like the village of the boy. And the graves of ancestors on the hill beyond the village? Do they destroy graves?

"What village, Uncle?"

The old man, squinting into the light, gave the soldier the name of their village.

"Near what town?"

"Dongduchon."

There was a pause.

The flashlight did a quick slide and landed on the face of the woman. She closed her eyes.

"Who's this, Uncle?"

"She is my wife."

The flashlight lingered a moment on the woman and then moved to the boy.

The boy stared directly into the light. Small. Very small.

"Who's this, Aunt, your grandson?"

"Yes, grandson," the woman answered quickly.

"What happened to him?"

"His parents dead. Village burned."

"What's in the cart?"

"This and that from our house," the woman said.

He ran the light across the cart, letting it linger over the splintered wheel and then brushing it across the quilts. He took his time poking the quilts with the flashlight. The light narrowing and burying itself briefly and reappearing. A diminishing and vanishing and returning of the world.

The old man watched the soldier, and the woman leaned against the cart shivering and gazing at the fires on the plain, and the boy stood very still, feeling on his arm the small bony fingers of the woman.

Behind them the line of refugees stood in silence, dimly visible in the cold starlit night. Vehicles kept on along the road, an endless procession, all going north.

From somewhere in the darkness up ahead a voice called out in a strange language. The flashlight moved away from the cart and shone fully upon the face of the old man.

"Uncle, have you relatives in the North?"

Almost everyone had relatives in the North. But the North was the enemy.

"Ah, yes. An uncle and cousins. Uncle long ago gone to his ancestors. Cousins I do not see since I was a boy."

"Aunt?"

"No relatives in the North. All my relatives only in the South."

He shone the flashlight again upon the boy.

"What's the matter with him?"

"Very bad wound," the woman said.

She opened the boy's jacket and shirt. He gasped as the cold air bit his flesh.

In the harsh beam of the flashlight the healed wound had the look of violated flesh.

The soldier turned his face away and waved them on.

The old man bent to pick up the shaft of the cart.

"We have no food," he heard the woman say.

"Trucks come in the morning with food."

"We have no food for tonight," the woman said.

In the darkness up ahead the voice called out again in that strange language. The soldier replied and the voice answered.

"Move," the soldier said to the old man.

"We will die without food," the woman said.

"Tell your woman to move, Uncle."

"Come," the old man snapped.

She picked up the shaft. The boy pushed from behind.

As they passed through the line of burning oil drums a soldier stepped out of the shadows and held up in front of the woman a small paper packet of rice. Without a word he dropped it on the quilts in the cart and then vanished back into the shadows.

They rolled the cart off the main road onto the narrow dirt path that ran through the plain. Its broken wheel now perilously tilting, the cart jounced and squeaked along the path and the boy tried to keep it raised so the wheel would not touch the ground. But after some while he thought his arms would come loose from his shoulders and he set the cart back on the wheel and pushed from behind. Then the old man came over to the wheel and lifted the cart and the boy took the other shaft and pulled together with the woman.

On the plain was a vast shantytown. Firepits and oil drums and makeshift shacks on the frozen ground and shadowy figures squatting or moving slowly about. Dark arctic-cold moonless air with currents of smoke and heat from the fires. Patches of brushwood humped and dwarfish beneath capes of snow. An odd noise over the plain: a low sighing and moaning ascending toward the black sky and pierced now and again by sharp clanging sounds from the military compound.

A patch of uninhabited darkness amid the surrounding fires: they left the path and settled the cart on it.

All around them shanties and huddled figures.

Quickly the old man shook snow from nearby brushwood and with the help of the boy loaded the A-frame while the woman with the last of her strength cleared snow from a section of ground near the cart and dug a shallow pit with the same stone tool the boy had used to make the hole in the pond near the cave. Digging, she wondered briefly why the ground was not frozen to stone. She put snow into a pot and when the old man and the boy returned built a fire and busied herself preparing the rice.

She thought: Who was he, the silent soldier with the gift of rice? One of the pale-skinned ones with the upside-down eyes? Sometimes kind and sometimes cruel creatures. Mother told me this how when she was a servant once in the house of the provincial governor and saw with other servants through finger holes poked in the paper doors and screens the governor dining with a pale-skinned man. Odd how he removed his hat when he entered the house. Ill-mannered creature. Mother said she learned from her grandfather that different kinds of creatures eat different kinds of foods, some eat stones, some wood, some grass, some water, some air, and the highest creatures, humans, eat rice and pork and raw fish, and the pale-skinned creature ate rice and pork and was clearly human even though his eyes were upside down and he removed his hat upon entering the house when it is known to all that a hat is put on to show respect not taken off what good is a hat as a sign of respect when it is not on the head where it belongs. Mother said that perhaps everything is upside down where they live, because they live on the other side of the world. Ah, look at the boy, my heart aches for the boy, he is so tired, he sits leaning against the cart exhausted, patiently waiting for his rice. And my man with the pipe in his mouth, hungry for his food. How will we sleep tonight? It is less cold here than it was in the mountains but it is still cold enough to kill us.

She offered the rice to the spirits of the plain and then served it and they crouched near the fire huddled in quilts, eating. Along the distant main road vehicles kept moving like squat yellow-eyed creatures, blacker than the darkness of the night, all heading north.

When they had eaten, the woman put the snow-cleansed bowls and pot back in the cart and returned to the fire.

"We will take turns again at the fire," the old man said.

"I will take my turn," the boy said.

"Are you too tired?" the woman asked the boy.

"I will go first," he said.

"Then you will wake me," the woman said.

"As you wish," said the old man.

"And I will wake you."

"I hear what you are saying."

"How will we sleep?"

"We should make walls of two of the quilts and sleep under the cart. And if we die, we die."

"We will not die," the woman said. "That is not a way to talk."

"What the spirits decide to do, they do," the old man said.

The boy helped the old man spread the pads and quilts and unroll the sleeping bag on the ground between the wheels of the cart and then drape two of the quilts over the four sides of the cart.

"You are sure you can take a turn?" the woman asked the boy. "Because if you are too tired you should not."

"I am not too tired."

"Remember to wake me."

The old man was putting more wood on the fire. Flames leaped in the windless air. He gazed out across the plain. Flat, treeless. Prickles of cold dread crawled along his back. Something here.

The woman moved into the space beneath the cart and slid into the quilts. She lay back and felt a sudden rush of iciness pass through her. From what? A creature of piercing cold residing in the ground? She shivered and began to rise but her fatigue held her like a stone weight and she was asleep before the old man slipped in beside her.

He thought: This wall of quilts will not help us much

against the cold. How bitter if death comes tonight after all we have been through.

The boy sat by the fire inside a quilt wondering what the old man would have answered had the soldier asked him instead of the woman, Who's this, Uncle, your grandson?

Why am I so cold with the heat of the fire on my face? So close to the flames and yet still shivering. The air so still, black and silent air, cold and smelling of raw earth. As on the night of the campfire in the forest when I dared the boys of my chronological group to cover me with earth to see how long I could stay under the ground and the earth was cold and dank on my nose and eyes and face, smelling of moist roots and wet stones, and I lay there so long Badooki began to whine and scrape at the ground and they rushed to uncover me and I climbed out laughing and brushed the earth from my clothes. Breathing through a reed they couldn't see in the dark. And after supper Father called me to him and said, giving me a hopeless look, This is a foolish boy, how is it I have in my house under my roof such a foolish boy? And Grandfather said, The boy likes to explore, there is a curiosity in him, one must know the difference between a boy who explores for understanding and one who explores for excitement only. The second is foolish and dangerous. Which are you? Grandfather asked me, and my father replied, I say this is a foolish boy and one day his foolishness will cause him harm, may the spirits protect and guard him, what will you do next to shame me in the village, foolish boy? And he turned away from me very angry. But Grandfather kept smiling around the long stem of his pipe. Who told Father? No doubt fat and greasy and loose-tongued Choo Kun. Dead all of my chronological group. Ashes all their homes.

There is something strange about this place. Fires burning everywhere except on those two patches of darkness and where we are now. Big black circles and all around them fires, and fires all around the Americans, are they warm the Americans, I was warm in my village with the smoke from the kitchen fire running under the floor and our sleeping pads on the floor, the heat baking us no matter how cold outside. The old man and the woman, they must be very cold if I am cold so close to the fire. The old man doesn't like me, I don't know why, no matter what I do he doesn't like me, I'll go back with them to their village if the Americans drive out the Chinese and the soldiers of the North, and then I'll go to my village, someone must still be alive, they couldn't all have been killed, I'll live with an uncle, a cousin, how could they all have died?

Is it already time to wake up the woman? I'll stay a little longer. Six times with the fire tonight instead of five, were we really in the mountains last night? let her sleep, some fires have gone out, will there be many dead of the cold here in the morning? Badooki once found a man dead in the forest near our village, a stranger dead in the snow, no relative of anyone in the village, and no one would touch him, no one would take the responsibility of the funeral, and finally someone called the police. Badooki barked and we all came running, all in my chronological group, we were playing in the forest, and the man lay very still, not still the way you are when you sleep, but the way a stone is still, or a sack of grain, dead stone still, and fat greasy Choo Kun stared at the body and turned green and went away to vomit. I told my sisters to have a look at the body and they screamed and put their hands over their mouths and ran frightened into the courtyard beside the garden. Ah, girls.

How many times have I added wood to the fire? I can't remember. Let her sleep.

He sat shivering inside the quilt. I made a tent of quilts once in the forest with my two little brothers and we slept in it near the campfire, all dead my little brothers, hands bound and earth in their eyes, they kill children too, why do they kill children? what did children do to them? told them stories of ghosts that night, wandering ghosts, Badooki in the tent lying next to me warm, and stories about the two stars, the wandering cowboy and the weaving girl meeting only one day a year, on the seventh day of the seventh moon, because the cowboy had neglected his cows and the weaving girl her weaving, so they were punished and must forever live separated by the Milky Way, each person must tend to the duties in his proper sphere, a story Grandmother told me, I felt it a duty to teach my little brothers what was being taught me, but they only wanted to hear more stories of wandering ghosts, and there were mosquitoes and fireflies in the tent and the smell of the forest, and suddenly it began to rain, a waterfall of rain came through the trees, collapsing the tent and sending a river down on our heads, and Badooki ran around barking and we laughed and collected the wet quilts and ran and Badooki barked and followed us into the house and he was so wet, we all looked at him and laughed, and I called him Two Three, he was so small and wet, all his fur gone, and we slept on the floor in the house, my little brothers and Badooki and I, how long ago was that, how long, I can't remember, how many times have I put wood on the fire, I can't remember.

He fell asleep and woke with a start and then dozed and woke again. Shivering, he heaped wood on the bed of glowing embers and watched it catch fire and burn high and saw the snow had melted near the firepit and the earth oozing tiny rivulets despite the dense curtain of glacial air that lay upon the plain. Time to wake him, he thought, dazed. It must be time by now. Is that light coming from the sky or from the

American compound? How warm they must be. And the food they have. Wake the old man, wake him, it must be time.

The old man moaned but woke without a word. Staggering slightly, he went to the fire, where he sat in his quilt staring into the flames, still inside his troubling dreams.

The boy lay down beside the old woman and was instantly asleep.

Gunfire from the American compound woke the old man from a half-sleep: three shots in swift succession. He experienced a confusion of frightful images: the Chinese, the soldiers from the North, the woman, the cart, run, run. Rising, he tripped over an edge of the quilt and nearly tumbled into the fire. He scrambled to his feet, his hands touching soft muddied earth, and stared wildly around at the fires and the darkness across the silent plain and the cloud of reddish light over the American compound and the line of military vehicles moving along the road. Trembling, he piled more brush on the fire and sat inside his quilt listening to the beating of his heart.

In a haze of shivering bewilderment and fatigue, his head feeling oddly weightless and his eyes seeing the fire as flaring halos of yellow light spreading from the center of the flames, the old man thought he remembered the woman telling the boy to wake her but he could not be certain or perhaps the boy had tried to wake her and she would not rise or the boy had forgotten or the woman had not said that to the boy, she had said to wake the man and the man was to wake her, she would be angry again if he did not wake her, perhaps the boy had waked her and I dreamed the boy woke me when it was the woman who woke me, the dreams were strong tonight, dreams of planting the seedlings, with my feet in the hot brown waters of the paddies, the soil oozing out between my toes and the woman beside me or with the ox and the sun beating down upon my shoulders, and in the evening the rich smell of the

fields and the cool breeze from the mountains and the moonlight on the wrinkled face of the river, strong dreams tonight,
Uncle said a man before he dies dreams of the best moments
of his life and carries those memories on his journey into the
next world, he told me while we hunted pheasant in the mountains with a hawk, three-year-old female bird, beautiful plum-
age, Uncle trained her himself, she lived in a thatched-roof
birdhouse in Uncle's backyard, sat perched on a branch six feet
above the ground staring out at the world, a leather thong
looped around each of her legs, a cold cruel untamed look in
her glittering eyes, on the hunt the hawk sat on the thick
leather glove that protected Uncle's muscular hand, we crossed
a river and climbed a steep hillside and saw a farmer plowing
a patch of cleared earth with an ox, and Uncle said to me, Is
that what you want to do or is this? and he raised the hawk
high over his head and the hawk fluttered her wings and the
bell on her back rang and later, as the hawk swept across the
valley like a swift shadow in pursuit of a pheasant, Uncle said,
pointing to it, That's what I want to remember, that's what I
want as my last memory to take with me on the journey to
the next world.

The old man stirred and roused himself and heaped more
wood on the dying fire. Light already in the sky? Figures
beginning to move about. A child crying. The muted wail of
a woman: someone dead of the cold? Gray curling mist, vague
distant hills, pale blurred sky. Melted snow around the fire,
the ground oozing water and mud. Raw brown seeping earth.
Strange.

He got to his feet, the quilt still around him, and took
some steps away from the fire. In the faint light of the predawn
sky he bent down and scraped snow from the ground and
probed the land with his fingers. Miniature hills and vales.
Rough earth, knobby, recently turned. He prodded the

ground: not quite frozen, yielding. Scooping out a handful of earth, he put it to his nostrils, smelled it, let it sift down through his fingers, sensing its texture, watching it fall.

He stood and looked around, then walked some yards to a low dead fire outside a nearby shack and bent and put his hand on the snow and scraped it away. Here the earth lay like solid rock beneath his fingers: hard-packed, unturned, frozen, winter earth, not the earth on which he and the woman and the boy slept, not that earth, a different earth.

He rose slowly and returned to the cart, walking with care. Drawing the quilt about him, he squatted next to the cart on the side where the woman slept. He sat there staring across the plain, waiting for the sun to rise.

The woman woke from a dream in which she had been tending the fire and a shower of sparks had ascended to the black sky and formed a constellation in the shape of the boy. She had been gazing up at it in wonder and love when next to her the boy stirred in his sleep and softly moaned, waking her.

She rose slowly, feeling the pain and stiffness in the joints of her arms and legs, and found herself in the dimness formed by the walls of quilts, staring at the underside of the cart. Old scarred unpainted pine cut and planed and built years ago by the carpenter.

For a long moment she could not remember where she was.

Emerging from the quilt draped over the side of the cart, deep wrinkles of sleep on her face, the woman saw the old man squatting near the cart and gazing across the plain. She started to speak but the words stopped in her throat. She hawked up morning phlegm and spat into the snow.

He shook his head, an abrupt gesture.

She followed his eyes across the plain.

The fire was down to a bed of gray-white ash and a few glowing embers. A morning calm lay upon the plain like the hush of a new beginning, and over the ground a cottony mist through which the orange fires on the American compound glowed dull and diminished. Here and there a figure moved, ghostly in the mist. On the main road, trucks, jeeps, half-tracked vehicles, ambulances: wheels and engines oddly muted in the morning stillness. Large dark birds with outspread wings sailed slowly in wide circles across the milk-white sky.

The woman stood looking out at the plain. Did the boy wake me or did I dream it? No, he woke me, as he said he would. Strange I cannot remember waking beneath the cart during the night or sitting in the cold. Did I dream that I tended the fire or did I tend the fire and dream the boy in the stars?

A cold wind blew silkenly across the plain. The mist began to rise.

Slowly the floor of the plain opened out to her eyes.

She saw the mounds immediately and then the shanties that crowded the plain. Two low snow-covered mounds: each roughly circular and about fifty feet in diameter; each at opposite ends of the plain. Odd protrusions bare of shanties and people. Directly upon the circumferences of the mounds began the world of the refugees. Remnants of metal and canvas made up the walls and roofs of most of the shanties: parts of trucks, jeeps, tanks, half-tracks: bent hoods, rusted doors, twisted fenders, pieces of armor; burn marks etched into them, narrow gouges, a welter of scrapes and scratches, vague tracings of numbers and words.

The woman followed the old man's gaze as it moved across the plain and back to the cart and then to the land behind the cart. She saw they were near the center of the plain at the edge of a huge mound of snow-blanketed ground that rose irregularly to a height of about six feet.

They were the only ones encamped on the mound.

The path through the plain briefly touched the rim of the mound and then wound on. Along the other side of the path and from the rim of the mound as far as the eye could see stretched shanties constructed from the wreckage of military vehicles.

The old man thought to wake the boy and move the cart.

At the far end of the plain four trucks left the road and began to move toward the American compound. Instantly all up and down the plain the air stirred and there were shouts and cries. Figures emerged from the shanties and hurried toward the compound.

The old man went over to the cart as the woman woke the boy.

"We are going for food," she said. "Stay with the cart."

"Hurry, woman," the old man called.

The boy came out from beneath the cart, blinking.

The old man and the woman, carrying bowls and pots, rushed off in the direction of the compound. The boy stood leaning against the cart, staring open-mouthed at frantically moving swarms of people.

He threw brush onto the dying embers and as the wood caught he turned and saw the rise of the mound behind the cart. Then he looked again across the plain and shivered. After a while he squatted near the cart inside a quilt, trying to make himself very small, and waited for the old man and the woman.

Before they returned two other families moved onto the mound, not far from the cart.

The old man thought they should eat first and then search

for a new location, and as the woman cooked the rice three new families appeared. They were coming in off the main road from the region of a distant battlefield, hundreds of new refugees, speaking a dialect the boy found difficult to understand. He watched them set down their possessions on the mound. There were children among them, boys and girls about his age.

The woman called him and the old man to the fire. She offered the food to the ghosts of the mound.

"I have thought about it," the old man said. "Here it is less crowded. Why should we move? Did you see what is out there? Worse than the mudflats on the riverbank."

He took up his bowl. The woman looked away.

"This is a time of war, woman, and besides others are here now too."

They squatted by the fire, eating, and glancing from time to time at the mounds on the plain.

The old man was thinking: Many villages of the land may be here soon. Perhaps the boy will come upon someone from his village and go off with them and we will finally be rid of him.

The woman thought: This is a terrible place. Is it not forbidden us to stay here? And if we stay, can we calm the ghosts?

And the boy: There are boys and and girls here of my chronological group playing in the snow. There are no dogs here and and why do those birds keep flying in circles overhead?

All that day new refugees entered the plain and for lack of space settled on the mounds.

The old man and the boy scoured the plain and found the site where the battle had been fought: an area of about one square mile filled with the debris of shattered vehicles. They made three trips and brought back with them scraps of metal and a strip of filthy canvas pitted with tiny shrapnel holes and they built a shanty around the cart a little more than double its length. A stink of muck and grease and fire clung to the metal. The fourth wall of the shanty had a space in its middle about the width of a man and faced out on the firepit.

The boy had found a length of frayed rope and he and the old man worked together trying to repair the wheel of the cart. But the rope snapped.

In the afternoon the boy went off alone and was gone a long time. The woman sat by the fire with the winter sun on her wrinkled face and the man, his pipe in his mouth, squatted near the shanty. When the boy had not returned by sunset, the woman rose and stood silently, watching, and the old man brought a quilt and covered her shoulders and stood next to her, staring out at the plain.

The boy returned at twilight. They saw him emerge from between two shanties waving over his head a length of thin black wire he had found in the earth amid the wreckage. The old man was surprised at the surge of relief he felt. Together he and the boy repaired the wheel while the woman cooked supper.

They slept that night in the shanty. The boy woke the woman for her turn at the fire.

Alone by the fire in the early hours of the morning the woman boiled water and cooked rice and set out the rice in a bowl as an offering to the suffering dead of the plain.

She bowed her head. No peace ever for the soldiers who lie in these mounds, a kindness to feed them. No roast pig to offer them as we sometimes did at the yearly ghost worship in our village. Only this rice. Let it calm your suffering. I will offer it to you again each night for as long as we are here.

She sat through her hours of the night.

The fire burned low. She heaped on brushwood and got to her feet and went to the shanty to wake the old man.

The old man squatted by the fire and noticed the bowl of rice. He shivered and drew the quilt tight about him.

Closing his eyes, he listened to the night and was certain he could hear echoes of the battle once fought on the plain.

He remembered his relief at seeing the boy emerge from between two shanties at twilight and was astonished to discover that he liked his memory of the day spent with the boy building the shanty. Warm in the shanty under the sleeping bag and the quilts. The boy curled close, reaching out in sleep. Wispy touch and weight of his arm, a thin bony arm resting with floating lightness on my chest. A small boy, and clever. Smiling and waving the wire over his head. Helping repair the wheel, helping return the cart to life. Good spirits in him.

The old man squatted by the fire watching the dawn come to the plain.

6

Before he woke the woman he ate the rice in the bowl by the fire. Her offering: but by now the ghosts have surely eaten. He chewed slowly the glutinous ball, tasting it on his tongue and feeling it slide down his throat and into his stomach. Gone for a while the stabbing pain of hunger; and strength to collect brushwood for the fire. Two fires, we need another fire to soften the ground in back. The woman and the boy will not go hungry, the food trucks will come again.

He scratched at his chest and crotch and then, holding the bowl in one hand, reached beneath his cap with the other and searched through his hair. The itching on his scalp grew so intense he thought to bring his head close to the flames. But it subsided under his furious scratching and he sat back on his haunches, eating with pleasure, his scalp and chest faintly tingling.

A wind began to blow from the north, shaking the flames. He shivered: cold air burrowed through his clothes. Odd wind-borne sounds came to him: cries of children, women wailing, pebbly tire noises from the vehicles on the road. A sudden acute memory of dissimilar morning sounds. In the village the birds would set up a clatter of song and the dogs barked and the cows and oxen lowed. Sometimes the old carpenter would have come back from a night of drinking in the marketplace with his cronies and the old man could hear him moaning and his crippled wife talking to herself and to their pig about the life she might have led had her father agreed to marry her off to the smart young student from the nearby village instead of to this carpenter, the son of her father's old friend. Good with his hands, the carpenter. Wise about many things. But too often drunk on warm rice wine.

Through the gelid air a dull-gray light began to inch across the plain. Squatting by the fire, the bowl in his hands nearly empty, the old man thought he heard whispers and snow-crunching footsteps and he looked up and saw the night dead being removed from some of the nearby shanties. Men and women and even children silently carrying their dead wrapped in cloth or canvas. Moving cautiously through the melancholy light. From one an arm dangling. Where do they take them?

He finished the rice, slipped quietly into the shanty, and put the bowl into the cart. Warmer in here. Let them sleep. The boy like a little child. Not long ago nearly dead. Saved by the dog. Young smooth face, a baby's face. Maybe a dog might have saved ours. No dogs anywhere on this plain. Maybe the boy's magic will bring us another dog.

He took the stone tool from the cart and quietly went with it outside, behind the shanty, where he scraped away the snow and dug a shallow pit. He put wood into the pit and built a fire. Then he returned the stone tool to the cart and woke the woman and the boy.

Trembling with the pain and fatigue in her arms and legs, the woman went outside and stood still a long moment, gasping for breath in the wind. She walked carefully on the frozen snow to the back of the shanty and squatted down near the new firepit.

The old man slipped the A-frame over his shoulders and went off with the boy.

Squatting, the woman saw them moving between fires and shanties toward a distant line of brush and scrub oak along the near foothills bordering the plain. As she watched, two helicopters flew with fearful suddenness low over the main road on the rim of the plain. She could see clearly their large red crosses and she raised her arms in vertical and horizontal motions. To bring on good spirits, Mother said. One this way and one that way. Good spirits of the earth and sky, good spirits of the valleys and plains. Up and down, and then this way and that. Mother learned it from the pale man with the upside-down eyes who ate in the great house of the governor. Many learned it from him. And songs too. *Have thine own way Lord have thine own way thou art the potter I am the clay.* Mother taught me.

She stood and went to the fire in front of the shanty and filled a pot with snow. She caught herself humming the song as she put the pot on the fire. *Have thine own way Lord have thine own way.* The wind blew stiffly across the plain. Low dull-gray clouds threatened snow.

With their bare hands they shook snow from clumps of brush and tore off branches and piled them on the A-frame, which sat on the snow beneath a low oak. From where they stood they could see much of the plain: its three mounds now mostly covered with shanties, and the American compound with its perimeter of wire fence and fire, and the hills that enclosed the plain in a nearly perfect circle.

They worked quickly and in silence, shivering in the merciless wind. The way we gathered wood in the forest when we camped in the winters with Badooki, bend the branches back and forth, break them, pull. Pick the ones with lots of shoots, more to burn. Thin fingers like a girl but he works hard and knows what to do. Fat greasy Choo Kun taught me that, he was good for something. Loose tongue and big appetite. Earth on his tongue now. What will we do with him, he is not of our blood? Perhaps ask the carpenter? Yes, another load for the second fire, you remain with it here, I will return for it. See how many are tearing at this brush. Like locusts. All along the foothills. How much wood is there on this plain? And when the brushwood is gone, what then? Perhaps the winter will end before the wood runs out. But if not? What is the boy doing? Ah, clever boy.

The boy had brought with him the torn pieces of rope, whose ends he had tied together, and the length of wire left over from the repair of the wheel. These he slipped under the second pile of wood and knotted tight, leaving extended ends which he now used to lift the brushwood to his back and loop over his shoulders in a makeshift A-frame. Together they started back across the plain through masses of huddled people and scampering children.

The woman saw them coming toward her walking slowly beneath their loads. Her heart went out to the boy. Where is his strength from? A few days ago nearly dead and now almost bent double beneath such a load, like the man, but the man has a back of iron, the boy is like grass.

The old man dropped his load of brushwood near the firepit in front of the shanty; the boy took his inside and placed it next to the cart. Leave it behind the shanty and someone will steal it. His stiffened hands burned. He thrust the numbed reddened flesh under his armpits. The fingers tingled and throbbed and curled. This is a foolish boy, Father said, only a very foolish boy exposes his hand in such a way to snow. Mother gently bathing the hand in warm water. Grandfather said, smiling around his pipe, Now that you know what can happen to you with snow, will you try it also with fire? Shall I tell you what the Master said? The Master said, Only the wisest and stupidest of men never change. Which are you? He is a foolish boy, Father said, and I fear for him.

The woman was calling him. He went outside and sat with them at the fire. Before they began eating, the woman offered the rice to the ghosts of the mound. The flames roared and smoked and crackled in the wind.

After they had done eating, the woman cleaned the bowls and the boy went into the shanty and brought out wood for the rear firepit and then scraped a hole in the softened earth. As he squatted he saw a group of boys about his age running past a nearby shanty. One of the boys extended his arm in a blurred shadow of motion and a shirt left to dry on the roof of the shanty was suddenly gone.

The boy stood up and covered over the hole and went to join the old man and the woman inside the shanty.

In the late morning the trucks came again and the old man and the woman rushed off toward the American compound.

They hurried across grimy snow frozen by the wind into ridged sharp-edged hillocks. Swallowed up inside a surging crowd, they felt themselves climbing a distance of ground and then descending: they had traversed one of the mounds. The woman, fearful of being separated from the man, walked behind as if one flesh with him, matching her every step to his. She thought: It is colder here now than it was in the mountains, there is nowhere to hide from this wind. Will the little house be enough for us? The man thought: If we come late and the food is gone I will die and in the morning I will be the one they will carry away. How they push, like animals at the trough. Do these trucks come every day? See that little boy, eight or nine years old, how he slips his hand into that man's pocket. He is stealing his spectacles! Vanished into the crowd. Nothing in my pockets. What will a child do with spectacles? Trade them for food?

A mute shivering mass of people stood near the trucks and edged toward the tailgates, where uniformed Koreans doled out rice from opened sacks. Fifty yards beyond the trucks rose the wire fence of the American compound. Near the gate to the compound stood a small silent crowd of young Korean women.

The old man and the woman held up their bowls.

"Only one bowl each person," shouted the Korean on the truck.

"We have a boy," said the old man.

"One bowl each person, Uncle."

"But yesterday three bowls," the woman said.

"Not enough today. One bowl each person."

They turned away from the truck, holding the bowls tightly to themselves, and started back across the plain. The old man was angry and did not know at whom to direct his anger and that made him angrier still.

"I will give the boy from my portion," the woman said.

"Watch how you walk," the old man said. "If you fall we will all be eating from one bowl."

Far behind them a column of black smoke began to rise from the plain but they did not see it.

The boy was sitting in the opening of the shanty near the firepit watching three girls about his age playing the rope-skipping game, when the column of smoke appeared. Intent upon the girls, he did not see it.

The girls were playing outside a shanty about twenty feet

from the boy. A middle-aged man and woman squatted near the firepit at the entrance to the shanty. The woman carried a child in a sling on her back. The man, dark hair wild on his bare head, face gaunt and stubbly, kept coughing and wiping his mouth with the sleeve of his winter jacket.

Dancing adroitly among the ropes held taut by two of the girls, the third girl, her coat and skirt hiked above her knees, seemed to float over the ground. She danced with the wind in her face, her high cheeks flushed and her dark eyes shining.

The boy watched in a trance. The girls in our village did not play like that in front of boys. Fat Choo Kun once said only peasant girls played like that. Stockinged legs showing bare above the knees. In our village the girls never wore bathing suits or went swimming during the day. No matter how hot the air. Nor would Father or Mother. Only the barbarous Japanese and pale-skinned foreigners did such things, showing their flesh to strangers. On hot nights some girls would bathe in the pond outside the village where the trees overhung the bank and sometimes two or three in my chronological group would steal out to watch them. Naked in the dark night, pale and wonderfully beautiful with the soft blue starlight on their satiny skin. Whispering and giggling as they floated and kicked and swam about quietly in the still water. And one night fat Choo Kun without warning any of us suddenly coming out with the snarling hissing roar of a leopard, so real my skin turned cold and the hair on my head stood up, and the girls screamed and scrambled wildly for their clothes and fat Choo Kun could not stop laughing, not realizing he had frightened them away from the pond forever. Fat greasy stupid Choo Kun.

The boy sat watching the girl dancing among the ropes. He did not notice the sudden dying of the wind as though a door leading to the plain had been abruptly shut. The girl danced on a while longer and then another of the girls took her place and after a moment slipped on the snow and fell backward. They all laughed and the boy laughed too.

Suddenly coughing uncontrollably, the man staggered to his feet and disappeared into the shanty. The woman quickly went in after him, the baby's head swinging forward and back with her movements. The boy could hear the man still loudly coughing inside the shanty.

He looked at the girl. She stood listening to the man coughing. The light had gone from her eyes and her face was stiff with fear. After a moment she followed the woman inside and the two other girls sauntered off.

The boy put more wood on the firepit in front of the shanty and then checked the fire in back. An odd smell hung in the air and he wondered what it might be and experienced a momentary dizziness and a sudden stabbing vision of the little dog licking at his wound.

Where are they? Haven't they been gone a long time?

He shivered and squatted down by the fire. Lost in the dance of the flames, he thought he heard someone call his name.

He raised his eyes and saw only the girl sitting in the entrance to the nearby shanty. The man had stopped coughing and she sat now gazing open-mouthed at the cloud-filled sky.

The boy heard his name called again and got to his feet and saw the old man and the woman walking carefully toward the shanty with the bowls of rice. He went to the woman and took her arm and helped her into the shanty.

The smell was inside the shanty too.

For a while the man squatted near the fire, warming his hands. Then he put his long-stemmed pipe in his mouth and closed his eyes. The boy went to the rear of the shanty to add wood to the fire.

The woman was filling a pot with fire-softened snow when she noticed people standing about gazing silently into the distance. She turned her head and saw the smoke.

The dense jet-black greasy cloud boiled into the air from the distant point on the plain where the nearly perfect circle of hills parted abruptly to open out into a narrow pass that led through a pine forest and a valley to mountains hidden in mist. The black smoke climbed, churning, to the low-hanging snow clouds and, its passage blocked, curled in upon itself like a huge dark angry flower and then opened and spread wide and drifted slowly over the plain.

At first the smell was odd and startling. Those who, like the old man and the woman and the boy, were seeing and smelling it for the first time stared in disbelief: what on this plain could be giving off such an odor?

The boy had come to the front of the shanty and stood near the fire staring up at the cloud. He saw the man and woman in the nearby shanty staring up too, the girl next to them. The old man sucked on the pipe and the woman turned away and began to busy herself with the rice. Then she put down the bowl.

The smell had changed.

Suddenly acrid, the smell entered the mouth and throat and nostrils and washed across the mucous membranes and lingered, leaving behind a coating that could be tasted.

Some put their hands over their mouths and noses and others covered their faces with cloth but the stench could not be staved, it penetrated and remained long after the cloud had gone. It clung to the rice the old man ate and the brushwood the boy heaped on the fires and the quilts with which the woman covered herself in the afternoon, when, feeling a weight of fatigue, she lay down to rest.

By then the old man and the woman knew what had been burning. But they said nothing of it to the boy.

The old man sat covered in a quilt beside the woman inside the shanty and the boy stood near the entrance, which he had covered with a quilt, watching the girl, who was again playing the rope-skipping game with her two friends. How she skipped and danced over the ropes! She saw him watching her and hesitated a moment, then turned her back to him and went on with the game. After a while they tired of it and the girl went inside.

In the evening it began to snow.

All night it snowed and through much of the next day, forming drifts that buried some shanties and toppled others. Those who had died during the night were carried away in the morning through the snow. The food trucks did not come and the old man and the woman and the boy ate the rice balls the woman had prepared and stored from the ration of the day before. There was no black cloud that day, and no stench of iodine and roasting meat.

The old man and the boy rose early and struggled through the blowing snow and gathered brush and hauled it on their backs and stored it in the shanty. They let the fire in the back die, saving the brush for the fire in front. With the frayed rope and the piece of wire, the old man tied lengths of brush together into a kind of broom and he and the boy took turns using it to clear snow from the roof and the area around the firepit.

In the late afternoon the old man lay down to rest and the boy labored alone to keep the weight of the snow off the roof. He saw the girl trying to push snow away with her hands and he offered her the brush and she took it from him with a murmured thanks.

The next day the sun shone and the food trucks returned and at noon the black cloud boiled up again over the plain.

❖

Later that day the old man walked through the snow to the adjacent shanty. In front of the narrow blanket-covered entrance, between two scarred and bent pieces of olive-green metal, he noisily cleared his throat. He waited a moment and again hawked and this time spat into the firepit. But the smell of the black cloud would not leave his mouth.

The blanket was drawn aside and the girl stood in the entrance, looking up at him out of frightened eyes.

"Tell your father a man wishes to speak with him."

The girl disappeared. The blanket, frayed and moldy, fell back across the entrance.

Waiting, the old man heard a dry deep-chested cough from inside and thought: A man with such a cough does not live long. He stood before the entrance, shivering in the wind.

The blanket was again drawn aside, abruptly, this time by the man.

"I and my family live next to you," said the old man.

"What do you want?" He had a hoarse, agitated voice. "I have nothing."

"Do you have any tobacco?"

"I don't smoke cigarettes."

"For my pipe."

"I have no tobacco, I told you I have nothing."

The two men regarded each other for a long moment.

"Well, come inside," the man said, and coughed.

The blanket slid shut behind the old man.

"Your fire is low," he said.

"The woman is ill, and the girl is a child, how much can she gather?" He ordered the girl to add wood to the fire. "Not too much," he said.

She slipped quietly from the shanty.

Dusty light filtered through a torn piece of dirty white

cloth covering a narrow jagged tear in one of the metal walls. In a shadow-filled corner squatted the woman, holding the child in her arms, eyes lowered as the two men entered and sat down on the grimy blanket in the middle of the earthen floor.

The old man dimly made out the woman's face: long, gaunt, ugly; a squat nose, thin cracked lips, a bony chin. A skeletal face on the man: high cheekbones; deep irregular trenches crossing his forehead and webbing his eyes and cheeks; thin spittle-flecked lips. He wore a dark jacket and wadded white trousers, and sat with his hands under his thighs, shivering and coughing, surrounded by a nimbus of exhaustion.

The girl re-entered the shanty. The old man felt the wind carrying the stench to his nostrils. Silently the girl sat down next to the woman.

"I have other things besides tobacco," the man said.

"For tobacco I have things to trade."

"Then there is nothing to talk about."

"What other things?"

"What have you to trade?"

"Pots. Bowls."

"We have pots and bowls." The man coughed. "Who can eat pots and bowls? Can I feed my family pots and bowls?"

"I have other things as well."

"Tell me about your other things and I will tell you about mine."

"In such a place a man must warm his bones," said the old man after a moment.

"There are ways to fight off the demons of cold."

"Where is your village?" asked the old man.

"Our village no longer exists. The fiends from the North burned it to ashes."

A moaning sound rose from the woman. She sat rocking the baby and quietly sobbing. The girl put her hand on the woman's arm. Then she closed her eyes.

"My ancestors were farmers to the tenth generation," said the man. "There are four generations of graves. Once I had six children." He coughed and wiped his mouth on the sleeve of his jacket. "Have you children?"

"We have the boy."

"I see you together bringing the wood."

"Ah."

"It is difficult for the girl to bring wood." He coughed. "For me it is not possible."

A sudden start and cry from the child; soothing words from the woman. The girl, her head fallen forward upon her chest, had seemed asleep. But she stirred and raised her hand and softly stroked the child's face.

"What did you farm?" asked the old man.

"Mostly rice. And millet, beans, and barley. I had also chickens and pigs."

"The boy is a good boy. He is strong."

They sat a while longer, talking. The old man got to his feet and the other rose too, coughing.

"Take with you a gift from my house," the man said.

From a bundle of clothes and blankets he brought forth a bottle. The old man closed and opened his eyes and slowly nodded. He ran his tongue over his lips.

"Go in peace," the man said, holding back a cough.

"In peace may we meet again," said the old man.

Later that afternoon he sat in the dim shanty sucking on his empty pipe and drinking slowly from a bowl. Hunting black cock with Uncle in marshes and larch groves. Uncle shot a male bird. Snowstorms most of the day. He taught me how to use the gun and I tracked a hen through the marsh and caught her feeding on larch buds and shot her. This is from my nephew, Uncle bragged to those in the village hut that evening, holding high the hen. Young, but a good eye. Well, he said to me, well, a hunter or a farmer, what will you be? He owned a pony, some guns, and three bundles of this and that. That was all. Traveled around alone and now and then with his two sons. Hunting with rich Japanese and Russians and occasionally an American. Father was angry. A hunter! Disgraceful! We are six generations of farmers, not lowly hunters. You will not go anymore to visit your mother's crazy brother.

He sucked on the empty pipe and refilled the bowl and drank some more.

The woman looked at him from the quilts where she was resting.

"Why do you do that now?"

"It is to drive away the smell."

"This is not a time to become like the old carpenter."

"Woman, I cannot endure the smell."

She lay back on the quilts. Once the ghosts begin to destroy they harm the good as well as the bad.

"Where is the boy?" he asked after a while.

"Somewhere outside."

"He should not go off alone."

"You tell me the boy is not of our blood," the woman said. "Why do you care where he goes?"

She closed her eyes and drew the top quilt over her face. The stench was deep inside the quilts and no matter how she turned or breathed it would not go away.

He walked with the wind in his face, treading carefully on the befouled snow and trying not to breathe deeply the reeking air. The wind blew the black smoke directly across the plain, driving it into people's nostrils. Overhead the birds circled effortlessly on the wind and once in a while a helicopter burst across the sky, chopping at the air. A pall of exhaustion lay upon the plain. People huddled near fires: forlorn shadows in the chill sunlight. Only the young seemed still able to move about quickly.

Tears came to his eyes from the searing wind. He felt them on his cheeks. Everything here is frozen, why not the tears? Choo Kun said tears don't freeze because they flow from a secret hot pool deep inside our bodies and are really liquid fire. His father told him that, Choo Kun said. His father is a poet and a scholar, Grandfather said, and did not utter anything so foolish. His father: hands bound and earth in his eyes. Liquid fire. Fat dumb Choo Kun. Earth now in the secret hot pool deep inside him.

Boys about his age roamed the plain in groups of four or five, silent and stealthy, like gray shadows. He avoided them. Near the gate to the American compound he saw young women huddling together and heard them calling to soldiers who stood behind the wire fence. He could not understand their words. How had they so quickly learned the language? Inside the compound soldiers wearing gloves and parkas with the hoods tight on their faces moved among huge olive-green machines and trucks. One of the girls laughed suddenly and stepped forward to the fence and threw open her coat and blouse. Loud noises burst from the soldiers.

The boy, his cheeks flaming, turned away.

He started back across the plain. A cloud covered the sun and he looked up. Heavy and gray, from the mountains in the North. More snow. If the trucks do not come tomorrow how will we eat? Walking and looking up at the cloud, he did not see the group of boys coming toward him and nearly ran into one of them.

They were quickly around him: five boys about his age.

All his size and height save one, a tall scrawny boy with two missing front teeth, which gave his small thin mouth an odd cavernous appearance. He seemed to be their leader.

"Eyes in front, boy, not in the sky." No anger or threat in his voice.

"Very sorry, I apologize."

"What is your name?"

He told them.

"Where do you come from?"

He gave them the name of his village.

"You have your parents?"

"Yes," he said.

"Lucky. We don't have our parents. Parents dead."

They stood around him silently in a wind that was now unrelenting with the absence of the sun.

"We see you looking around."

"Is it wrong to look around?"

"You want to join us?"

"For what?"

They glanced at one another expressionlessly.

"You have something you want to trade?"

"No."

"You want to steal something?"

"No."

"If you steal something and you want to trade, you come to us. Don't go to nobody else. We give you the best trade. You hear?"

The boy did not respond.

"Hey, you understand? You hear?"

He nodded. There were tears in his eyes from the wind.

"I live over there." He pointed to a shanty near the American compound. "Okay?"

What did that mean, okay?

"You have a sister?"

"What?"

"A sister."

"No."

"Too bad. You could make lots of money and get food."

They stood looking at him in silence.

From their leader came a barely perceptible signal: a shrug, a quick motion of the hand. They hurried off and were gone.

He wiped his cheeks and eyes with the palms of his hands. Liquid fire. Fat greasy stupid Choo Kun.

The stench was out of the air. But it would be a while before it left his nose and tongue and throat.

He walked hurriedly back to the shanty, his eyes on the foul-crusted snow.

The woman squatted before the fire, preparing soup. In a twilight made duskier by the clouds that now covered the sky she seemed strangely insubstantial, a gray slow-moving apparition.

As the boy entered the shanty the snow began to fall.

The old man sat on the quilts, leaning back against the cart and sipping from a bowl. He squinted at the boy across the rim of the bowl and shivered.

"You were gone a long time."

"I walked to the place of the foreigners."

"Dangerous to go too far alone." He sipped from the bowl. "Uncle said even a hunter should not go off too far alone. Is the smoke gone?"

"Yes."

"I cannot endure the stink."

The woman entered with the pot of rice soup.

"It is snowing. We will eat inside."

"We need meat," the old man said sullenly.

The woman did not respond and offered the rice to the ghosts of the mound. She heard clearly the cries of the ghosts alone on the plain in the wind and snow. Homeless, wandering.

They ate in silence, listening to the winds driving the snow against the walls of the shanty.

In the morning the old man and the boy searched through snowdrifts for wood. Returning laden with brush, they went past the shanty of the girl.

The old man said, pointing to the brush on the boy's back, "The man and woman are sick. You can help the girl."

The boy said he would go with the girl to gather wood.

He went over to her later that morning. Barehanded, they gathered branches and heaped them in two piles and carried them on their backs to the girl's shanty and left them near the firepit. Shy and fearful, the girl murmured a word of thanks and disappeared into the shanty.

The boy returned exhausted, his stiffened hands cut and bleeding. He slipped beneath the quilts and lay very still, shivering. His thighs and back quivered and there was a dull pain in his chest in the area of the wound. The woman sat near a wall humming to herself. Leaning against a wheel of the cart, the old man snored softly, an empty bowl on his lap. Tired old people, the woman kind, the old man crude; ugly faces, not like the faces of Father and Mother. The boy held himself very tight and would not cry. Old and ugly and kind and crude and separating him from the orphans that roamed the plain.

They ate the last of the rice that night and in the morning the food trucks did not come. At noon the black cloud appeared again over the plain.

"If I had become a hunter I would know where to find meat," the old man muttered. "Don't tell me there is no meat on this plain."

He went to the nearby shanty and received a small portion of rice for his promise that the boy would again help the girl gather wood.

"This stink will kill me," he said later to the woman.

She did not hear him but hummed quietly to herself as she added wood to the fire. If there were meat I would offer it to the ghosts and they would stop sending the wind and the snow and the smell. But he is not a hunter and we have no meat.

Raising her arms, she made vertical and horizontal motions in the air and then sat very still, gazing into the climbing fire.

The trucks returned the next morning and after the old man and the woman left for the food the boy searched through the shanty and on the cart in the box containing the spirit of the old man's father he found the nearly full bottle. He went to the girl and asked her to keep an eye on the shanty and headed cautiously toward the American compound.

The group of boys his age and their leader were in the shanty near the compound. They would not let him inside. He stood in front of the entrance with the leader and handed him the bottle. They spoke briefly. The leader disappeared inside and after some minutes returned.

The boy walked quickly back and saw the black cloud begin its ascent.

Inside the shanty the old man sat in a rage on the quilts, muttering to himself, and when the boy entered turned to him abruptly as if to ask him something but seemed to change his mind and remained silent. Later he went over to the next-door shanty and after a while returned with another bottle and sat again on the quilts with the bowl on his lap.

The boy went with the girl to gather wood. When he showed her the gloves her eyes widened and when he slipped them on her hands she began to cry. Old thick gray wool. His were of animal skin, brown musty fur-lined. He looked at the tears in her eyes and thought: From some hot secret pool inside. Liquid fire. She let herself laugh a few times as they gathered wood and carried it back. Brief fleeting laughter. As if she feared the anger of the ghosts of the plain.

When the old man saw the gloves on the boy's hands he felt a burning fury. His vision blurred and his heart beat tumultuously. This is how he thanks me for saving his life. This thief, this deceitful child, this son of scholars and land-owners. Death to him!

He kept throwing fierce glances at the boy, who sat by the fire next to the woman. The boy had given her his gloves to wear for a while.

Later the boy brought the gloves to the old man.

He slipped them over his aching hands, feeling with a shiver their smooth furry warmth. The rage he felt began to yield to reluctant and envious admiration. This is certainly a clever boy. Good magic and very clever. Helpful to have in my house such a clever boy.

Some days later the boy woke in the early morning and knew a stranger was in the shanty. There had been a change in the air, a sudden flurry of cold, and he had sensed it inside the quilts, sleeping beside the woman. Who was at the fire in front? The old man. Probably asleep. Or maybe he was in back, tending to his needs.

Raising his head from the floor pad, the boy saw with a shock the girl silhouetted against the drawn-back quilt at the entrance.

She stood very still as the wind blew around her into the shanty. The boy could only dimly make out her features but he saw that she was not wearing her gloves.

The old man slid behind her and came inside, lowering the quilt and shutting out the wind.

She stood there, silent, rigid, her eyes wide and her mouth tight.

The woman woke and sat up. After a moment she went over to the girl, speaking to her softly. She reached out and put an arm on the girl's shoulder and the girl cringed.

The old man and the boy went past the girl and walked in the snow to the nearby shanty. Inside, the woman sat on the floor, moaning softly and holding the baby. On a blanket on the floor lay the body of the man.

The girl appeared in the entrance.

The old man and the boy stood looking at the body. He seemed already part of the earth on which he lay.

"Help me," said the girl.

The old man stared down at the body and ran his tongue over his dry lips.

"Help me," the girl repeated.

"Put on your gloves," the boy said to her.

The old man wrapped the blanket around the body. When he covered the man's face the woman broke into a wail and the girl sobbed and the baby began to cry.

They lifted the blanket-wrapped body, the old man at the shoulders and the boy and the girl at the legs. Its weight seemed to the old man surprisingly light, as if its most substantial element had been the spirit that had made the body its brief home.

The woman's wail rose and the baby was still crying when they took the body from the shanty.

Outside stood the old woman, watching them with despairing eyes. Others glanced at them and looked away. They carried the body past the firepit and started with it across the plain.

Through the gray air a north wind blew minute crystals

of frozen snow like darts against their faces. A brief climb across one of the mounds with the wind in their mouths and eyes left them breathless and they put the body down and rested. The girl's raven hair blew about her face and eyes and she was crying and the boy saw the tears on her cheeks. The old man stamped his feet and blew on his hands and the boy offered him his gloves, which he took, and they lifted the body and went on.

The old man thought: And who will carry me when I lie stretched out like that on the earth? The woman and the boy? Or strangers? See how the boy labors. Skinny but strong. And cunning and resourceful. Such a boy may be of help to me and the woman.

And the boy, feeling his hands growing numb, thought: What will she do now, she and her mother and the infant? What happens to them when they lose a father? Who helps them? Spirit of Grandfather, protect me. Protect the girl. Where are we going? Does the old man know where to take us? We have gone past the Americans. Girls there talking to the soldiers, laughing. How could she do that, open her clothes that way to the Americans? So many gangs of boys roaming around. Will it snow again? There are others walking too, carrying their dead. And all going to the same place. Where? She is still crying. Tears on her cheeks. Wet. From the hot secret pool deep inside her? Dumb Choo Kun. Rest again. The old man is very tired. Is he sick? I'll go out later alone and gather the wood for us. If *he* dies. If the woman and I have to carry *him*. Where are we? Here is where the plain leads out to the pine forest and the mountains. What is that there? *What is that?*

A large length of charred earth lay before him, black against the snow. Heaps of scorched twisted shapes darkened grotesquely the frozen ground. Carried by the wind were traces of the stench brought by the dirty cloud. People filed past the blackened earth and averted their gaze. It took the boy a long moment to realize what he was seeing and then his knees buckled and he fell and the girl fell almost on top of him. The old man, unable to hold the body, let it slip to the ground. The girl was crying silently and trembling. The old man helped the boy and the girl to their feet and they picked up the body and went on to a stretch of frozen earth where two Korean soldiers with face masks were silently directing the placing of the dead.

They put the man on the ground alongside another man. The old man removed the blanket and began to drape it over the shoulders of the girl, but she drew away and he folded it and gave it to her instead. One of the soldiers shouted at them to move on. The boy made horizontal and vertical motions with his arm over the man. The soldier shouted at them again. As they walked back across the plain the wind died and the sky began to clear.

Later the trucks came and the old man and the woman went for their food. At noon the black cloud rose and curled across the sky. The boy saw the girl and her mother standing at the entrance to their shanty, staring up at the cloud. He wanted to talk to the girl but did not know what to say.

The next day the boy walked over to the girl's shanty to help her gather wood and found it empty and everything gone. It seemed so tiny, a dwelling for dwarfs. Why had they left? Why had the girl said nothing to him? Not a word, nothing. The old man shrugged and turned away when the boy told him and sipped from his bowl; the woman shook her head and bent lower over the soup she was preparing.

Soon there was another family in the shanty, sullen people from the coast, not given to talk.

The boy roamed the plain, seeking the girl. One day he

thought he saw her with others of her chronological age but when he came near it was only a girl with gloves like hers. Where could they have gone? On through the forest toward the mountains? Along the road back to the war? Or had it all been a kind of dream? The girl, the man, the woman, the infant. The way the cave seemed a dream to him now and the mountain pool and the little dog. And his village and Mother and Father and and Grandfather and his sisters and brothers and and Badooki and fat Choo Kun and his idea about tears and and and . . .

The old man's bottles were not a dream. He seemed possessed of an endless supply.

Some weeks later the Americans suddenly moved out. They packed their gear, loaded their vehicles, took down the wire fence, and left behind a large rectangular empty space. Their jeeps and trucks rolled across the plain and joined the other vehicles heading north along the main road.

For a few days the area where the compound had stood remained empty and then some shanties appeared on it and in a week it was as though the Americans had never been there.

The food trucks came sporadically. But nearly every morning a jeep drove across the plain carrying American or Korean soldiers with odd-looking tanks which they strapped on their backs and soon the black cloud would appear.

Then Korean military police turned up and ordered the area of the compound cleared. The old man and the woman were waiting in line at the food trucks on the morning bulldozers cleared away abandoned shanties and scraped the ground smooth and clean. A day later a new battalion of Americans arrived.

As the boy continued wandering back and forth across

the plain in search of the girl he again saw young women waiting at the entrance to the compound and orphans running about in packs and at times he wondered if he and the old man and the woman would end their lives there. Why had they been given back their lives if all they were to have was the life on this plain?

The days were now longer, the winds gentler, the ground softer. The snow had begun to melt. The dead were buried in the earth and the jeep no longer came and the cloud and stink were gone.

One morning a wave of sound rolled across the plain, a rippling motion, a stirring, and men and women came rushing back from the food trucks. The boy, squatting by the fire, heard the noise of a thousand murmurous voices and rose in alarm, and then he listened to the words and felt the sudden thunderous beating of his heart.

The old man and the woman returned, their faces flushed and their voices high. The woman prepared a soup and rice balls. They slept little that night and the next morning shook out the quilts and the sleeping bag and rolled up the strips of canvas and put into the cart whatever pieces of the shanty it could carry. They looked around and saw the emptying of the plain. The woman left an offering of rice in a bowl inside what remained of their shanty.

At noon they began the journey back to their village.

BOOK
THREE

7

In the mountains the air was cold, the dirt road still hard, but runnels trickled in the drainage ditches from the hours of high sun warming the snow. Straggles of refugees on one side of the road, foot soldiers in single file on the other, jeeps and trucks and half-tracked vehicles, and ice and snow on the headwalls and slopes above the timberline.

And once a long convoy of ambulances.

The woman looked at the red crosses on the ambulances and the old man saw her begin murmuring to herself but was unable to hear her words. They helped us, these spirits of the cross, together with our own, how does one give them an offering? Is it enough to sing their song? *Have thine own way Lord have thine own way.* What do they mean, these words made by the foreigners? Mother said the man who taught the words did not explain them clearly. Rare to teach a song in the language of the foreigners. The good spirits who like those words should receive an offering of thanks. I will think what to give them. Now see where we are. Strange, this was not the road we took when we came through these mountains. I didn't see the place where we slept. How did we miss this road when we left the valley? Were we so weak and sick we didn't even see ourselves take a wrong turn? And there were footsteps on that other road. Whose?

She shivered with a cold that was not from the air and together with the old man continued pulling on the shafts of the cart.

The boy pushed from behind. He kept looking around, thinking he might find the girl and her mother amid all the others. He thought they might come up behind him and he would turn his head and they would be there, the girl and the mother and the child. The girl still wearing the gray wool gloves. Sometimes he walked some steps with his eyes closed and formed a picture of her and was certain she would be there when he opened his eyes. He tried walking longer and longer with his eyes closed and her picture inside, and once he fell and skinned his palms: he had given his gloves to the old woman. In the late afternoon, after looking at the faces of many girls her age, he realized she reminded him of his little sisters and the girls of their chronological group with whom they would play on the swings. Up and down and up and down and very high and higher still and laughing. He saw the faces of his little sisters dead in the earth of his village and he shuddered and leaned forward into the cart and pushed hard and the old man called to him to ease up. This old man does not want me to live with them, he sees me as trouble, I don't know why, the woman wants me to live with them but she cannot win against the old man, I will return to the village, someone is alive, surely someone is alive, it is a dream sent by bad spirits that they are all dead.

The road climbed slowly into the mountains and the ice on the summits flashed white and blue in the late-afternoon sunlight. To the right the side of the road fell away in a steep drop and the old man, glancing at the narrow valley and frozen stream below, remembered the hawk soaring across hills and valleys after the dog had startled the pheasants into flight and the echoing calls of his uncle and cousins as they kept the hawk in view and raced to get to it quickly after the kill because if it gorged itself it would not hunt anymore that day. They would let it eat a few mouthfuls before putting the pheasant into the hunting bag. We caught five pheasants that day. The steep sides of the hills and how we ran up and down them sweating in the November air. Chasing the hawk chasing the pheasants. This is better than sweating behind a plow, Uncle said as we all sat in the warm hut eating two of the pheasants. Tell me, what do you think, will your father let me make his little boy into a hunter?

Glancing down the hill, he saw the gutted remains of a vehicle among ice-covered boulders below and now and then what he thought was a body crusted and frozen into an odd shape and fused with the ice of the slope and once all that remained of a pony. Some time before sunset the road began to run level and then descended sharply and the old man and woman felt the cart sliding downhill and pulled back hard on the shafts. Hurriedly the boy moved between them and angled his back against the cart. The wheel slid perilously close to the edge of the road and sent shards of frozen earth and snow down the slope. An ambulance passed and then a jeep, slowly, in whining low gear. Then the road leveled and ran on, embowered with murky air between the walls of towering hills. A while later they entered a narrow valley where people were making fires and setting up their shanties for the night.

They found a small flat rectangle of space near a tree and the old man tried to clear away the snow but found it frozen. Strange, on the plain the earth has begun to soften but here it is like iron. He and the woman spread strips of canvas on the snow and then he hoisted the A-frame onto his shoulders and went off toward a stand of pines to gather wood.

The boy helped the woman set up the pieces of metal for the shanty and began to dig a firepit with the stone tool. His fingers and hands smarted under the icy touch of the stone and snow: the old man had taken the gloves. He scraped frenziedly at the snow, feeling pain again in the region of the healed wound. The air was cold but without the burn of weeks before. All around him were fires and shanties and the smells of cooking food. Children roamed about in small shadowy groups. Slowly he shaped the shallow pit. When the old man returned the boy made the fire and the woman cooked the last of the rice and offered it to the spirits of the cross and the valley and after they were done eating the man sat near the fire sucking on his pipe and drinking slowly from his bowl.

"There is no stink in this valley," the woman said after a while.

"It is to keep warm," he replied sullenly.

"How many more bottles did you steal from them?"

"Hold your tongue, woman. We are returning home, where women know when and how to speak."

She turned away from him.

The boy sat in silence, staring into the fire. He felt the old man's eyes scrape his face and kept his eyes on the flames. I am nothing to him. He speaks to the woman as if I am not here. Father never spoke that way to Mother. Not when I was near. Look at him, he is going to become drunk again and the woman will not be able to wake him, and she and I will once more have to share his turn at the fire.

The woman sat thinking: The war has changed him, he was never this way before, a little rice wine in the town with his cronies but never night after night like the carpenter. How his eyes shine in the firelight. What does he see? The village? The ox? What memories? Foolish old man, if the war does not kill him, the drinking will, and his eyes will soon see the color of cold wormy earth.

The old man sipped again from the bowl and felt the hot

liquid inside him and wondered why he was still so cold. He shivered and saw clearly the glide and swoop of the hawk and the brief struggle of the pheasant. A cry of triumph burst from his uncle's lips and echoed through the valley. Do you hear that echo, asked his uncle. Do you hear it? From his mouth vapor plumes rose into the brittle November day. I have given this valley a special name. Echoland I call it. All the sounds of this valley run together into one great echo, a song that is sung by all the spirits of this valley. Only a hunter hears it. The spirits of this valley are happy when they see a hunter who loves the animals he hunts. A truly great hunter is grateful to the birds and animals he kills, he takes their spirits into himself. See all the things you can learn from me if only your father will let you.

He remained squatting by the fire drinking and after a long while he thought: I see the boy's eyes, he is clever and crafty, I have seen how crafty he is. It might be useful to have him in our home but not for too long, because he will begin to think that one day he will take my place, take my land and my inheritance and replace my name with his and perhaps not bring offerings to my spirit, because he is not of my blood, and make of me a shadow, a melting snowfall, a fading echo.

He fell into a drunken sleep by the fire and the woman and the boy carried him into the shanty and covered him with the quilts. The boy saw the shame and resignation on her face and looked away. After a while she lay down silently beside the old man.

The air was very cold but still. Squatting inside his quilt by the fire, the boy was thinking of the girl with the woolen gloves. If I find her will she and her mother come with me to my village? He could not remember the paths he had traveled across the hills and paddies to the main road and he wondered how he would find the village. The woman will help, yes. He pulled the quilt tighter about himself, suddenly frightened. Vague echoing sounds rose from the darkness. Hungry dogs? The furry spirits of the cave in this valley where he and the old man and woman had lived?

He sat watching the fire and from time to time tossed fresh brush onto the flames.

Crossing the valley the next morning, the woman looked for the cave but there were so many caves she could not be certain which one it was. The boy, pushing the cart from behind, squinted in the sunlight and thought he recognized the screen of brushwood they had placed in front of the cave opening: it lay covered in snow and ice with thin black fingers of brambles protruding from it. Walking beside the woman and breathing with difficulty as he pulled the cart, the old man had no interest in the cave: his head ached, his tongue felt gritty and swollen, there was a taste of cold metal in his mouth. He heard the boy calling from behind the cart: Could they stop and see the cave?

The old man said morosely, "I do not want to stop."

But the woman said, "Can it hurt us to see the cave?"

"Woman, I do not want to see the cave. Why should we stop for the cave?" Anger and warning filled his voice.

Still the woman persisted. "A visit to the spirits of the cave. An offering of thanks."

The old man thought: See how he delays us. He thinks the longer he is with us the safer he will be. A clever boy.

Without waiting for his response, the woman began to pull the cart to the edge of the path. The old man, raging within himself, felt it unseemly to resist her in front of the boy. They turned off the path and went on some yards over rocky terrain. A newly risen wind blew against the towering walls of the valley. They left the cart near the brushwood screen and approached the cave.

The woman stepped inside. Cold earth-smelling dimness and the silence of a tomb. This was almost our grave. She murmured softly to the spirits of the cave. Standing beside her, the boy saw in memory the pond and the fish and the three dogs and the old man dying on the cart.

The old man stood shivering in the entrance to the cave and would not enter. This was a place of weakness and shame for him: he had almost died here. He turned to go back to the cart and saw two boys, dirty-faced urchins, lifting out of the cart a rolled-up strip of canvas and a quilt.

He shouted.

Startled, the one carrying the quilt dropped it. They ran off with the piece of canvas.

The old man stood trembling, his shout echoing through the cave, the tiny furry creatures fully roused and flying about in a chittering frenzy.

"Woman!" he called.

The woman and the boy followed him back to the cart and they left the valley and that night slept inside a grove of shell-torn trees. Near evening the next day they set up the shanty on a mudflat at the edge of the sea.

A shivering wind blew in across the water. The light was slowly fading from the clear sky. Earlier that day a Korean officer riding past on a jeep had tossed the woman a packet of rice. Now the old man saw her cooking a soup. The boy stood near the fire, feeding wood to the flames.

She had dropped the shaft and stepped into the middle of the road in front of the approaching jeep. The old man and the boy shouted at her at the same time and the jeep skidded to a halt, the driver cursing, and the woman had pleaded for food and the officer had tossed her the rice. Stubborn crazy old woman. This will end when we return to the village. Such madness will cause her death one day and who will cook and mend and wash and help with the fields?

The old man moved across the mudflats to the edge of the sea. He stood on a curious swerve of shore, its shape the palm of a pleading hand, thin curled fingers protruding into the waves. Long crestless swells rolled in across the fingers. On occasion a wave rose languidly and crested and crashed against the shore, where it hissed and foamed before sliding back into the water.

As he stood watching in the last of the light a surging wave disgorged a school of tiny silvery fish.

He stared in astonishment: six fish flopping about and writhing on the ground at his feet. Glancing quickly around, he saw he was alone.

He waited until the fish were still and then scooped them up and quickly chewed and swallowed two and brought the remaining four to the woman, who took them from him without a word and dropped them into the steaming soup.

Before he fell asleep the old man whispered fearfully to the spirits of the sea: What are you saying to me with this gift of the fish? Is it about the boy?

The woman, lying beside him, did not hear his words. She murmured her thanks to the spirits that had sent the officer to her. Remembering the driver's anger, she said silently into the darkness: Could I let the boy go without food? A mother does not let her child go hungry.

Outside the shanty the boy sat huddled in a quilt, guarding the fire and the cart.

The next day they entered the city on the edge of the sea. A dusty brown cloud lay over the broken houses and streets, and soldiers patrolled amid the ruins. Men and women stood around burning oil-drum fires or squatted near shanties, and children played in the debris. The boy, staring with horror at the destroyed city, remembered his village. He had given up searching for the girl; he would return to the village without her. The woman kept murmuring to herself as they passed through the city and the old man smelled the acrid stench of burning that clung to the gutted buildings and remembered the stink on the plain and wished he had not finished off the last of the bottles the night before. Our village will smell like this.

They passed the barbed-wire fence of the airfield and the old man could not remember where he had been gathering brushwood when the guards had fired at him. Searching for the woman and the boy, the dread of having lost them, his memory of that now angering him. Let him return to his own people; let him take his cleverness back to his own village.

The advance of the Chinese and the soldiers of the North had been halted near this airfield and the dead had littered the road. Pieces of shattered military vehicles still lay scattered on the sides of the road and in the fields.

Before twilight they arrived at the riverbank in Seoul.

Quickly they set up their shanty and the old man went off to gather firewood. The woman laid out the pads and the quilts and the boy dug a firepit. Both banks of the river were crowded with shanties. A cold wind blew across the mudflats but its ferocity was gone. Ice floes clotted the surface of the river: scraggy leprous water creatures that frightened the woman. I will offer them the little rice we have left. May they not waken until we are far from here.

The old man had taken the A-frame and gone up the sloping mudflats and between two of the houses that faced the river. He saw the streets were bare of ice and now the houses had people living in them. There were people in the streets and some regarded him with suspicion: a withered old man with a wispy graying beard roaming about with an A-frame on his back.

At the courtyard with the broken stone wall where the

pile of wood had once been concealed, he stopped cautiously and stood looking up and down the narrow street. The wind that blew now between the houses made only the palest of sounds. There the little dog had entered the street; there it had stopped to eat the grains of rice; there from behind the stone wall he had thrown the first stone at it. How he hungered for meat. It was a ceaseless gnawing in his belly and his bones. Hunting with his uncle, he had eaten meat day after day. The best of foods, Uncle exulted. Do not roast it too long. For your strength and manhood, for that thing between your legs. Makes it big and hard. Meat.

He stood waiting near the broken wall. The street remained empty. Were there people now in the houses? He stepped through the break in the stone wall and entered the courtyard.

The pile of stones was still there. He stared at it, dazed. Clearing away some of the stones, he saw the wood.

He felt himself begin to tremble. The wood, the dog, the fish, the second dog, the second fish, again the wood. Is this the magic of the boy?

He set the A-frame on the ground, loaded it quickly, covered the wood with rocks, hoisted the A-frame onto his back, and stepped out of the courtyard into the street. This empty street. Inhabited by ghosts kindred to the boy? His father and mother? His grandfather?

He felt the hairs rising on the nape of his neck as he hurried down the street toward the river.

The boy helped him make the fire.

The woman heated the leftovers of the rice soup and fish they had eaten the night before and offered it to the spirits of the river.

They sat near the fire.

The woman pointed to the river. "There I carried you on the ice."

"I barely remember," the boy murmured.

"The doctor said he had no medicine to waste on you, you were already dead."

"I died and returned from the dead?"

The old man put down his bowl and shivered.

"Death had its hands on you," the woman said.

"I remember little from the time I was on the road running until the time I woke and saw you."

"You were more with the spirits than you were with us," the woman said.

The old man felt terror.

"Finish your food," the woman said. "Soon we will be in our village."

"Do you want me to remain here?"

"You will come with us."

The old man scowled. "Woman."

But she ignored him and spoke directly to the boy. "We will decide later what to do with you."

The old man made a low growling sound.

"One does not abandon an animal one loves, let alone a child," she said.

Early the next morning they left the riverbank and came out onto the wide main road leading from the city and walked with many others going north. Scarred stone buildings lined the sides of the city road: walls pocked by shrapnel; moldy canvas and splintered wood planks for windows and doors. Temporary power poles and restrung overhead lines. An occasional civilian bus lumbering along in the heavy flow of military traffic. Snow on some trees and black ice and snow on the road and gray gaseous dust rising from the street into the still cold air.

On a street where most of the buildings had remained intact they passed a two-story gray stone building with a flight of wide steps leading up to a portico. Over twin wooden doors hung a sign in Korean which said the building was an orphanage run by an American church organization. To the left of the building stood a tall wire fence topped with four strands of barbed wire. Children milled about in the yard behind the fence. Some girls were playing the rope-skipping game. Boys leaned against the wire fence, staring out at the street. How did I not see that when we came past here before, this is where we should have left the boy; is this where he wishes to leave the boy, in a place like this? One boy about ten or eleven stood with his fingers clutching the wire and watched the boy go by with the old man and the woman. Walking behind the cart, the boy had the sudden odd sensation that *he* was standing behind the fence looking out at the boy beyond the fence going past with the old man and the woman. An icy leaden grayness invaded his chest, a trembling dread, a sense of the cold earth of a grave. Do they live always behind the fence? What do they eat? Does anyone visit them? How much of their lives will they spend in that empty world? He tore his eyes away from the fence and the boy and concentrated them upon the cart. Small cart, old wood, splintered, scarred. Quilts, sleeping pads, pots and pans, pieces of metal, the box containing the spirit of the old man's father. He walked behind the cart, pushing it along the crowded road.

The city fell away. Fields and paddies on both sides of the road and looming snow-covered hills. Everywhere shanty villages had sprung up; people dwelling in the rubble of their past lives. The war had burned up the countryside; no town or village stood. Shacks and shanties and huddling people, and wood burning in oil drums, and children running about in packs, and here and there a starved dog and an ox. The old man and the woman and the boy moved slowly because of the traffic. There was snow on both sides of the road and snow on the fields and paddies and a thin haze of yellow-gray dust floated high over the road and dulled the early-afternoon sun.

They stopped to rest awhile. The old man and the woman fell asleep sitting against the cart and the boy gently woke them. Shortly before sunset they came to the place in the road where they had found the boy.

Along both sides of the road the fields were gouged with deep craters partially filled with pools of half-frozen black water. Scorch marks on the nearby hills: wide swaths of charred earth the snows had somehow been unable to conceal. The old man thought he could still smell the burning.

"There," the woman said, pointing to the drainage ditch where they had stumbled upon the boy.

"I can't remember," the boy said, feeling ashamed.

"It is better that you can't remember."

Looking down into the drainage ditch, the old man thought: The ox is gone. Nothing of it remains. See how they took even its bones. Just like our own ox. Nothing. If not for this boy I could have taken a piece of that ox and not have become sick later. He has been a burden and the woman has behaved like a stubborn animal and this will end when we return to the village. The spirits of our ancestors protected us from harm. But there remained annoyingly the thought that perhaps he and the woman had been saved by the spirits guarding the boy. How could he know which was true?

The woman said, "Here I carried you from the ditch and there, down the road, near the turn, I stopped the car with the red cross and the driver gave me foreign medicine for your wound. You remember nothing?"

The boy shook his head with shame and embarrassment.

"How hurt you were."

The old man was impatient. "Woman, the sun will soon set."

"We should stay here tonight."

He glared at her, raging. "Why stay here? We are not far."

"Can we enter the village at night? Who knows what waits for us?"

Delay and delay. One after another. She plays the same game of wait and postponement. They think it will help the boy.

He followed behind the cart as the old woman and the boy pulled it off the road and along an embankment over the drainage ditch and brought it to a flat area away from the craters. Others were setting up shanties in nearby fields. Shivering, the boy saw the sun slowly dropping behind the hills. With the shadows came a bitter cold.

The old man went off toward the foothills for wood, and the woman and the boy searched with their fingers in the icy mud of the drainage ditch and found roots and crayfish and last-season rice seedlings for the woman to make into a soup.

A light snow fell during the hours the boy sat guarding the fire and the cart and he felt the flakes on his face and tongue. Badooki would bark at snow and snap at flakes as if they were flies. Fat Choo Kun said snow was the spirits shaking out their quilts. He would run around in the snow scratching himself. Fat dumb Choo Kun. The night was dark, the noise of the traffic loud, did it never end, the traffic of the foreigners, day and night, did they never run out of cars, what were the roads like in their land, always noise? In time he woke the woman and she in turn woke the old man, who fell into a deep sleep near the fire and saw himself and his uncle hunting wild boar in the mountains of the North.

A helicopter woke him, flying in low from the hills and

over the valley and the road, going south. He jumped to his feet, listening. Was that gunfire? Had the war returned? Or echoes of the boar hunt with his uncle? You will not go there again, Father had shouted. He is a crazy man. He tries to steal you away from me. Unheard of. Does he not know common decency? This is the family of your mother, a man who does not know the order of things. A knife to him!

He stood there a long moment, dazed, and then woke the woman and the boy. Wearily they loaded the cart and rolled it across the fields to the road.

Heavy military traffic going both ways. Ugly shanties in the fields and along the sides of the road. Clinging yellow dust underfoot and in the cold sunless air. The cart jounced, the boy pushing from behind. Was the wheel tilting again, the wire coming loose? Black ice and grimy snow in the roadside drainage ditches. Pulling on the shaft, the woman recalled the large town they had passed along this road during the flight from their village: homes and sheds and markets. A blight of shanties now across an expanse of cleared scarred mucky earth. The foreigners saved the country but the North destroyed the land. Will we live now our remaining years in a shack made of pieces of metal and wood? Can the spirits be so without mercy?

The road crossed over a wide culvert and the old man saw four tanks moving quickly between the fields, hatches open and commanders on the machine guns, shields yellow and brown with caked mud, long cannons pointing north, clanking caterpillar tracks kicking up dust. If the soldiers from the North did not burn the village, the big machines of the foreigners certainly crushed it. To rebuild the house and the shed. Where will we find wood in this burned land? How many of the animals survived, surely they took all the animals, those barbarians. And is the old carpenter still alive?

The road twisted and curved awhile and ended parallel to the railroad tracks that ran north from Seoul. At the crossroads about a mile south of the cart path to their village there had been a town, a train station, and a large marketplace. As they approached the town, the woman saw the marketplace: once big, attractive, lively, now a squalid strip of thrown-together shanties along the side of the road across from the railroad station. The station platform and its protective overhang, gone; now only flat bare earth. Shanties from the edge of the tracks and on into the foothills behind the new one-runway airfield on the other side of the tracks. Across from the airfield the main road branched off at right angles into a road that went past the end of the marketplace into an American division compound. American soldiers lounged near the market stalls talking with Korean girls. Jeeps and trucks rolled in and out of the compound. On the runway a single-engine aircraft buzzed with power, rolled briefly along, and leaped into the dim air.

The woman stared in astonishment at the marketplace and the airfield and the compound. On the shaft next to her the old man was looking about in disbelief. The air seemed so lifeless, the light melancholy and filled with shadows. He felt in his heart the desperation of the land. The boy, remembering his village before the fire, recalled a tale told him by his grandfather about the illness sent by the spirits to someone who went around gossiping and telling mean tales about others. I said something cruel about fat Choo Kun. The spirits sometimes punish an evil tongue with an evil illness, Grandfather said. It seemed to the boy that everything here had caught that illness. Had the land been so evil as to merit this punishment by the spirits? The land near the village of the old man and the woman had become leprous.

About a hundred yards beyond the crossroads lay the entrance to another compound: long low buildings and tents and jeeps and trucks, and vehicles with huge red crosses. Seeing the crosses, the woman raised her arms in vertical and horizontal motions. Some distance after the wire fence of the compound they stopped on the side of the road near a cart path.

The boy came out from behind the cart and stood in front of the old man.

"This path leads to the village," said the old man to the boy.

The boy lowered his eyes.

"You can stay with us awhile but then you must leave."

The boy felt his heart freeze.

"You are not of our blood and there is no place for you in the village."

"After all we have been through," the woman said.

The old man wanted to say: Perhaps I will ask the carpenter whether the boy can stay with us. But the thought that the carpenter might agree filled him with bewildering dread. When in his life had he been so fearful of another, especially a boy?

He picked up the shaft.

The boy followed behind the cart as it crossed fields and paddies and began a gradual climb to the crest of a low hill. He could not see what lay below the crest but in the distance beyond the crest was the sloping rise of another hill which flattened into a long shoulder before leading down gently to unfarmed wild-grass fields that went on to the wire fence of the American compound where the trucks with the red crosses stood.

On the crest the old man and the woman brought the cart to a halt and stood gazing down. The boy thought they would continue on in a moment and waited behind the cart but when they had not moved in a while he came forward and glanced at their faces and realized they were looking down the hill and followed their eyes and saw the village.

It lay at the end of a small round valley beyond rows of

terraced paddies. Winter trees and courtyards and sheds and grass-roofed earthen homes. Two girls on a see-saw near a wall: flowing red and blue skirts green and yellow blouses long red-ribboned pigtails. A woman walked along the village path, a bundle on her head. From some of the chimneys rose white smoke.

The woman began to weep soundlessly and turned toward the hill, murmuring words of gratitude to the ancestors of the village. The old man felt the rising of the hairs on the back of his neck and the heavy beating of his heart as he stood staring at the columns of climbing white smoke. A confusion of feelings: soaring joy at the saving of the village; astonishment that they had survived; dread at the might of the boy. No doubt now. This is a boy with the same magic as the ginseng root. To have him in our home. Power.

They brought the cart down the slope and across the paddies and entered the village. The girls came down off the swing and hailed the old man and the woman and stared curiously at the boy. Men and women appeared in doorways and spoke quietly, glancing toward the hill.

The shed stood intact and the old man went inside but all that was left of the ox was an envelope of leathery skin and some bones crumbling into the earthen floor. A horrid stench filled the air and he backed quickly out. Take care of it tomorrow.

In the deep pit behind the shed the large clay vase of kimchi lay buried and untouched. But rats had nibbled away much of the rice in the two bags stored in the small shed attached to the animal shed. And nothing remained of the dried fish.

Murmuring her thanks to the spirits of her ancestors, the

woman entered the house. Tiny creatures skittered across the floor, leaving behind zigzagging hairline trails in the thick dust. The main room was cold and had about it the dank smell of the cave. Men and women began appearing in the doorway and speaking softly with the old man and the woman. Where? How long? Most of them farmers. Glances of wonder at the boy. Girls poked their heads in and looked at the boy and giggled.

Though it was only early afternoon the boy was suddenly very tired.

A man stood in the doorway, bantam and brown-skinned, deeply furrowed skeletal features, dark glittery narrow eyes, thick-fingered callused hands. He was bareheaded and wore a dark jacket and baggy white trousers and rubber shoes. His hair was white and a wispy white beard lay across his lips and chin. He looked very old and he gazed intently at the boy, and the old man went over to him and they stepped outside, speaking quietly.

The boy stood watching the woman clean the house. She brushed vermin from the walls and removed the straw mats and inspected the sliding screens and swept the floor. She told the boy where the wood was kept and he went through the kitchen and carried wood inside and put it into the stove. She lit the fire. The hot smoke, moving through the flues beneath the floor to the chimney on the other side of the house, began to warm the air.

The boy sat down cross-legged on the bare floor and leaned his head against the wall. Fire and ashes, my house. Tired. Am I sick again?

He fell asleep sitting on the floor and dreamed the house was on fire.

Someone prodded his shoulder. He opened his eyes and looked into the face of the old man.

The floor was baking hot. He rose dazedly to his feet.

"I will return to my village," he heard himself say.

"The carpenter is a wise man," the old man said. "He has been to many towns and has seen the cities and mountains of the North. He says it is a cruelty to send you away and you may remain as long as you wish."

"With respect, I will return tomorrow."

"You should remain until you get back your strength," said the woman.

"Remain as long as you wish," said the old man again.

Strange old man. Suddenly he wants me to stay. Why?

"The carpenter says you can work for the foreigners."

"With respect, I will remain until my strength returns and then I will go to my village."

"As you wish. In the meantime, if you should want to work for the foreigners, the carpenter will tell you what to do."

"I do not want to work for the foreigners."

"We must eat," the old man said. "Many in the village now work for the foreigners. It is not dishonorable."

"My mother was a servant in the house of the provincial governor," said the woman proudly.

"I want to go home."

"If your village is burned and all your people are dead, you have no home," said the old man. "Your home will be a house for children without parents or fields and roads and streets."

And the woman asked, "Did we save you for that?"

"I'm very tired," the boy said. He wanted to sit down on the floor and lean his head against the wall and go to sleep. *Why couldn't I find the girl? She would have gone with me to the village.*

The floor was hot. He felt the rising heat brushing his face and eyes. The woman went out to bring the floor mats inside. They had left the cart in the courtyard, near the tree. The man took from it the box with the spirit of his father and placed it tenderly against a wall of the main room. Through the doorway the boy saw the woman shaking out the quilts and running her hands over the corners and edges, searching for lice. She spread two pads on the floor and covered them with quilts. A third pad and a quilt and the gloves she took into the adjacent small room.

The man squatted on the floor, sucking on his pipe.

"I will bathe you," the woman said to the boy, "and then you will sleep."

"I am able to bathe myself."

"Of course you are. But now you are too tired."

"I am not a child."

"I don't know what you were before," the woman said, "but no one will ever say of you now that you are a child."

She drew water from the well and heated it in pots on the stove and the boy sat cross-legged and naked in a tub on the hot floor of the main room and she bathed his face and neck and arms, carefully avoiding the sores on his lips, and then began to wash his back and chest.

The old man sat on the floor, smoking his long-stemmed pipe and watching the woman bathe the boy. How thin he is, the bones sticking out from his chest and ribs. The penis and genitals look to be fine though the hair has not yet appeared. The years before the body changed: he remembered them dimly as if through a screen of dark smoke; the times of hunting with his uncle were clear. How gently she washes him. Nearly a grown boy and she bathes him as if he is a child. The child if he had lived would be a comfort now in our old age; grandchildren running about. The spirits decreed no. Angry spirits, we give them offerings all the time, with few results.

Stop, wrong thoughts, bring on their anger, stop thinking this. Maybe they gave us this boy in exchange, very strong power in him. See how tenderly she bathes him, his thighs and back and genitals. He lets her, he looks so tired. Singing. What is she singing? *Arirang, Arirang, O Arirang, The pass of Arirang is long and arduous. In the front of the house the young scholar is late at his books, In the rear of the house his neglected bride is weeping.* Old woman's voice. A good woman. But stubborn. The spirits were cruel to take away the child. See how she dries him now and puts on him an old shirt of mine and old trousers and rubber shoes and they laugh at the size. Do they play with us, the spirits? Are we their amusement? There is magic in this boy but he also brings with him too much re-membering.

The boy slept on a clean pad in the same room with the old man, and the woman slept in the side room. In the early morning, when the old man and the woman woke, the boy was still asleep. They moved about quietly so as not to wake him. When the old man returned to the house at noon after a walk through his fields and rice paddies, the boy was still asleep. He stood a long moment beside the woman, gazing down at the boy, and then went outside to bring more wood for the stove.

The boy slept a great deal in the weeks that followed but woke at odd hours during the night and lay listening to the dry noisy breathing of the old man and the silence of the village. No sound drifted here from the main road; the village lay in a shell of stillness surrounded by its low hills. Once he woke in the cave with furry winged creatures on his face; another time in the shanty on the plain, the air filled with the choking black cloud and the girl in the doorway like a beckoning ghost. He woke bathed in sweat and trembling, his heart beating ominously and the wound in his chest flaming with pain.

He rose late one morning and helped the woman bring wood into the kitchen and then walked about the village. Babies in the courtyards, girls on their swings, men repairing the paths and sluices in the fields and paddies, women cooking and washing. The village was smaller than his own: about a dozen homes, a single path, sheds, courtyards, trees. There were no boys his age: did they all work for the foreigners? And no animals. No cows, oxen, dogs. No chickens.

In the evenings, when people sometimes gathered in the house of the old man and the women, the boy listened to the talk. It was the talk of farmers. Weather. Plowing. No seed for planting. A lost harvest. Famine. Perhaps food from the government or the foreigners.

When they talked of the war, which was still raging far to the north, they lowered their voices and spoke in tones of fear. Villages all around them had been burned to the ground. Two of the farmers had lost their wives to hunger and sickness in refugee camps. One old man had been killed by an American bomb.

No one understood why their village had been spared. The boy noticed that whenever they talked of it some would glance at the hill beyond the village and murmur quietly words he could not hear.

He climbed the hill one afternoon in early spring and found burial mounds scattered about on the small flat areas of its tranquil slope; the broad shoulder was bare of graves and thick with winter weeds. He walked among the mounds awhile and then to the edge of the shoulder. Some distance below lay the American compound with its tents and long low houses and red crosses. Fine yellow dust floated across the compound from the traffic on the main road. As he watched, a small single-engine aircraft raced along the runway of the airfield and lifted itself into the air.

That night, as they sat on the matted floor after having just finished eating, the boy announced to the old man and the woman that he wished to return to his village.

The woman blinked and looked down.

"Perhaps wait a little longer," said the old man after a moment. There had been a promise of seed from the local government and he wanted the magic of the boy for the time of planting.

"With respect, tomorrow or the next day."

The old man went out to talk to the carpenter.

"So soon?" murmured the woman. "Are you strong enough?"

"The snows are gone, the weather is warm."

"I thought you would remain longer."

"If there is no one alive may I come back?"

She nodded gravely. "And if there is someone alive you will not come back."

"I will come back to visit."

"How I hoped you would remain a while longer," she said.

The old man returned with the carpenter. They sat down on the floor at the low table. A few grains of rice clung precariously to the carpenter's beard.

The old man spoke to the boy. "The carpenter has something to say to you."

"What I wish to say is this," the carpenter said in a strange whispery voice that seemed to be only air moving between his dry wrinkled lips. The grains of rice trembled on the wisps of his beard. "I wish to say that you should not leave the village now. In your leaving now I see much unhappiness."

The old man said, "The carpenter has been to many places and seen many things. He has been to the Shuotsu valley and the Tumen River in the North and to the great thousand-year-old temple of Buddha near Myokosan. He has climbed the sacred mountain to the Lake of Heaven and descended to the cave at the very center of the earth."

But the boy had not heard of any of those places and sensed an emptiness in the voice of the old man. Is he repeating words that are without meaning to him?

The woman said, "It is wise to listen to the words of the carpenter."

"Stay until after the planting of the fields," said the old man.

"I have seen in dreams the spirits of my father and mother," the boy said simply.

They regarded him with startled eyes.

"Twice I have seen them."

"What do they do in the dreams?" asked the carpenter.

"They speak to me but I cannot hear them or speak to them."

The carpenter shook his head and sighed. He tugged at his beard. Grains of rice fell onto his white shirt.

"Then you must go," he said.

The woman moaned softly. Give and take away. Cruel heartless spirits. The old man sagged. Fear descended upon him. The power gone. The world flat and empty. Dread of brutish demons.

"Do you know how to travel to your village?" asked the carpenter. A timbre of gentleness had entered his whispery words. "No? You will tell me when you are ready to leave and I will show you the safest way."

He rose unsteadily to his feet and the old man went with him outside.

"It will hurt me to see you leave," said the woman. A hole opening inside her. Cold and frightful darkness.

The old man returned. They sat together awhile on the matted floor in silence.

Two days later the boy left the village, carrying a packet of rice balls and a rolled-up quilt the woman had given him. He walked through the fields and paddies and turned onto the main road and followed it to the tall stone-and-steel bridge over the river. Flanked by muddy pebbled banks, the river ran dark and fast between tall hills. The original side spans were intact but the center had been destroyed and was now of planks that rumbled ominously as jeeps and trucks passed over them. A thin waist-high pipe railing lined the single narrow walkway. He held tightly to the railing and felt a chill weakness in his legs looking down at the water foaming around the bridge piers far below.

On the other side of the bridge the road descended steeply to the floor of the river valley and ran parallel to the riverbank. He passed men coming down from the hills carrying A-frames loaded with brushwood. No one took notice of him.

Months before, on the flight from his village, he had forded the river farther north but the carpenter had warned him the river was treacherous now for the melting snow. By noon he was sweating and he stopped in the thin shade of a new-leafed tree and ate one of the rice balls. The woman's eyes dark and moist as she handed me the packet and the quilt. Same quilt we used in the cave and later, but much cleaner now, she said, her mouth in a sad smile. The old man silent and sullen. Angry if I stay, angry if I leave. A strange old man.

Aircraft flew by overhead. Swift silvery aircraft very high; small fragile olive-colored aircraft; aircraft with whirling shadows on top and no wings. Machines on the ground and machines in the air. The foreigners seemed to have an endless number of machines. Do the machines have spirits? Do the foreigners live this way in their own land, machines everywhere?

In the early afternoon he passed a small house on the side of the road and saw three young women lounging near the open doorway and an empty jeep parked nearby. The women wore skirts and one was naked from the waist up. The boy, going by quickly, saw the light-brown rounded flesh and the darker circles with the nipples and felt his heart racing and a turbulent heat on his face and a strange gnawing in his groin. He passed directly in front of the house and none of the women even looked at him.

Later he turned away from the river onto a narrow path that climbed into the hills. Toward evening he found a small glade and spread the quilt and gathered brushwood and made a fire. He sat by the fire and ate another of the rice balls. After a while he fell asleep on the ground with the quilt wrapped around him and woke shivering during the night and heaped more wood on the embers and slept again until the sun woke him to the stillness of the early morning. He woke thinking he had heard his mother calling him and Badooki barking somewhere among the trees. He washed his face in the cold waters of a rocky stream and continued on along the path.

From time to time he caught a glimpse through the trees of the river shining in the sunlight. Keep the river in sight, the carpenter had said, and on your right. A wise kind old man. At night often drunk and loud. How did he learn so much?

He crossed a long meadow and came to a forest, where the path abruptly ended. A wall of trees. Oaks and larches and elms and pines. An open ceiling of branches and needles and cones and young leaves. The smell of cool moist shade. Soft damp floor of moldy leaves underfoot. Tall trees, gnarled spreading roots, fallen rotting hollow trunks, the scuffing sounds of his footsteps in the leaves.

He kept his bearings by carefully watching the trees. Find a tall tree far ahead, the carpenter had said, and walk to it and then find another tall tree. Watch where moss grows on some trees, it grows facing north. When you come to the end of the forest, turn right and follow the tree line. Soon you will see the pond you describe. Whispery voice. Like wind through a tube. Grandfather's voice nasal, deep. Mother's voice soft and sweet. Father's voice high. There, over there, a flood of sunlight and the end of the forest. Grassy hill running downward. Field mice in the grass and yes the willows and the pond, there, the pond.

Voices.

The pond, lying at the far edge of the broad meadow that bordered the forest, was separated from the village by a row of willows. Men and women along its rim, strangers; and shanties side by side. Stagnant yellow-green scum on the water eerily bubbling along the edge. A stench came from the pond, thick and suffocating, and the boy felt it seize his throat.

No one had seen him emerge from the forest. No one paid any attention to him as he walked slowly past the pond into the village.

Shanties one next to another on blackened earth still clotted with ashes. The ground mucky with urine and clogged with firepits. A babble-voiced hum from squatting men and women. Half-naked children waddling about. Boys about his age gathered in small groups, talking. Girls playing the rope-skipping game in the swirling dirt. The air thick with the stench of filth. He walked back and forth, dazed. Where was his house? Where was the courtyard where his mother and the maids had cut vegetables and mended clothes and his sisters and brothers played? Where was the next-door house of fat Choo Kun? Here and there the remnants of a house as part of a shanty: charred roof tiles and foundation stones; a splintered plank of red pine; a blackened roof beam. Is this my village? Did I take a wrong turn? But the forest is there and the pond. And the meadow. My gang of friends building bonfires in the meadow on the fifteenth day of the New Year. And and kite-flying in the spring and summer. And bathing in the pond under the autumn moon to keep away illness for the year. And and sitting on the bank and singing. And Badooki Three Four Two Three coming out of the water after a swim and shaking himself. And and and . . .

He walked frantically back and forth among the shanties, seeking a familiar face. People stared at him indifferently.

Outside the village he searched for graves along the slopes of the hills. Shell craters marked the earth and many mounds had been flattened. He could not find the graves of his ancestors.

He walked back to the pond. An old man stood urinating into the water, his phallus a wrinkled brown fat worm in the sunlight. In the forest the boy searched for the glade where he had once camped with his brothers and Badooki when the deluge had knocked down their tent of quilts. He could not find it.

He went on through the forest, first walking quickly and then at a run, and emerged at dusk and slept that night not far from the house of the young women on the riverbank. In the late morning he crossed the bridge and by noon he was back in the village of the old man and the woman.

The old man was working in the paddies when the boy appeared over the crest of the low hill near the village. Startled, he leaned on his shovel and squinted into the sunlight. The boy, his eyes fixed on the ground, did not see the old man. So soon back. And with a weight on his shoulders. The spirits of his village were uncaring and cruel. The boy's power will be used now only for us. Yet it was not triumph or exultation the old man felt on seeing the boy but a sorrowing pain he had never experienced before. He could not understand why he should feel that way and it troubled him.

In the house the woman lay in her room with an illness that had come upon her the day the boy left: a weakness of the arms and legs and a murmurous beating of her heart. She heard the boy's footsteps in the courtyard and then in the main room and rose quickly and greeted him. She brought him warm water and in the courtyard he washed away the grime of the journey and then in the main room he ate a bowl of hot rice soup and lay down to sleep. She squatted near him, murmuring to herself and making horizontal and vertical motions with her arm.

The next day the boy spoke briefly with the carpenter and the following week he went to work for the Americans.

8

The morning the boy left the village and walked along the dusty main road and entered the American compound for the first time the old man and the woman left their house and walked to their rice paddy and the woman with the old man watching slipped over her shoulders the harness of the plow. They began to harrow the field.

The plow was of wood and rope save for the curved iron blade and the woman pulled against the straps of the harness as the old man guided the plow with his hands on the shaft and the boy walked fearfully into one of the long buildings on the compound accompanied by a Korean soldier who brought him through narrow corridors to a small dimly lit room and told him to remove his jacket and shirt. The Korean soldier went behind a screen and the boy heard his voice. A tall American stepped out together with the Korean soldier and said something and the Korean soldier told the boy to stand in front of the machine that looked like a window.

The Korean soldier was a short thin man in his early twenties who wore an American uniform with foreign words on the shirt. He spoke commandingly to the boy. "Do not show the foreigner that you are afraid. This machine will look inside you to see if you have the lung sickness. If you have the lung sickness you cannot work for the foreigners. He is asking you to take a deep breath. No, no, breathe in, and do not breathe out until I tell you." The machine hummed and whirred. "Now you can breathe out. If they see shadows it means you have the sickness. That scar on your chest, where did you get it? Ah, you are lucky to be alive. Put on your shirt and wait here. If you do not have the sickness I will take you to your work. A nice jacket. Good cut of cloth. The carpenter said you are not of their village. Where were you born? Ah, sorry to hear. No one left? Barbarians. Listen, I'll give you a piece of advice, don't wear that jacket here, someone will steal it."

The boy waited in the dim room. Small. Make myself small.

The old woman pulled at the plow. A sudden sharp point of pain at the back of her head. She paused to run her hands over her sweating face and take deep breaths. A hawk circled high overhead, sailing slowly on currents of rising air. The warm spring sun and the paddy water nearly to her calves and the cool liquid mud between her toes. The rice seedlings will arrive too late from the authorities and perhaps there will be famine after the summer but the man said the power of the good spirits will help us. Now pain in my breasts, what is there in these dried-out sacks that can cause pain? The baby's fingers clutching, the lips suckling. Little mewling gurgling sounds. Good so good his tiny lips on my nipples and his little fingers touching and tickling the flesh. Here for a moment and suddenly gone. The man calls to me to go on.

An American in a white coat emerged from behind the screen and spoke briefly to the Korean soldier, who nodded deferentially. The American looked at the sores on the boy's face and wrote something on a piece of paper which he handed to the soldier.

The boy went with the soldier to another room, where an American behind an open window took the slip of paper and handed the soldier a small tube which he gave to the boy.

"Twice a day, morning and night, rub a little of this there and there on your face," the Korean soldier said. "It is the medicine of the foreigners to heal your face."

The woman and the old man had plowed nearly half the paddy by the time the Korean soldier and the boy left the long low building and started across the compound. Bare scraped brown earth, low brown buildings and tents, and a white building with a cross-topped tower at one end and rows of small canvas houses with curved roofs, and many jeeps and big trucks, and smaller trucks with big red crosses on them like the one the woman had said was driven by the Korean soldier who threw her the packet of medicine. Is he still alive, that soldier? Perhaps one should make an offering to his wandering ghost in case he is not alive. I will ask the woman.

The boy found himself being taken back to the entrance of the compound.

"Have I the lung sickness?" he asked, terrified. Once he had overheard his mother and father talking about a young uncle, a poet-scholar, who had died of the lung sickness.

"You do not have the shadows but you cannot work here until the sores on your face are gone. Come back in four or five days. Do you have the money?"

"Money? No. I have no money."

The soldier looked surprised and annoyed. "Four or five days. If the sores are not better you cannot work for the foreigners."

He walked away, leaving the boy alone just inside the entrance to the compound.

A cloud of yellow dust billowed up from the wide road. The helmeted soldier in the entrance guardpost looked at the boy.

The boy started down the road to the path that led across the fields and paddies to the village. Cresting the small hill that overlooked the paddies and the village, he saw the woman working harnessed to the plow. She moved slowly, bent forward, straining against the straps, while the old man guided the iron point of the plow beneath the water of the paddy. The boy went quickly down the crest and left his shoes at the edge of the paddy and felt the pondlike water and mud on his legs. Without a word he removed the harness from the woman and slipped it over his shoulders.

Behind him the old man loudly hissed his displeasure. "Scholars and poets do not work in the fields. Do you know what to do?"

"Will you teach me?"

"Today is not a time for me to teach you this. Give it back to the woman."

She reached out her small hands to the boy for the harness. Sweat bathed her face and he heard her panting breaths. His chest constricted.

"With respect, teach me."

The old man was in a sudden flaring rage. "You must obey me! How were you raised? A boy should know his place! I say to you, give it back!"

Cringing before the old man's anger, the boy handed the harness to the woman and retrieved his shoes and returned to the house. In my village I never saw this. An old woman pulling a plow.

Later that day he saw the woman squatting together with other women at the side of the stream behind the village, washing clothes and chatting. The war and the Chinese and the flight from the village. Where did they find the boy? The ditch the riverbank the sea the cave the mountain the plain. The fish the dog. She said nothing of the mounds and the black smoke and the smell. Talking, they beat the dirt from the clothes, pounding them with paddles on the flat rocks. The woman wrung the streamwater from the clothes and piled them still twisted in a bundle which she placed on her head and then returned to the house.

At night she made a supper of rice soup and kimchi and sat eating with the old man and the boy.

The old man wanted to know if the boy would be able to bring food from the foreigners and the boy told him and the woman about the window machine and the medicine for the sores on his face.

The old man puffed on his long-stemmed pipe. "I am a farmer, not a scholar." He sounded weary and vexed. "Tell me again what this machine does."

The boy tried to explain.

The old man was astounded. "This machine sees inside the body? The heart, the liver, the lungs?"

Frightened, the woman asked, "Does it see the spirits?"

"The soldier who was with me said it sees only lights and shadows."

"It cannot see the spirits," said the woman. "If the spirits could be seen they would be like us." She could barely keep her eyes open. Am I sick?

"We saw the spirits of the cave," said the boy.

"They appeared as winged mice only to our eyes," said the woman. "Can we ever know what the spirits really look like?"

"This talk doesn't interest me," said the old man. "It is the talk of women." He turned to the boy. "You must try to bring us food. Especially meat."

"I cannot return for four or five days."

"When you return you must bring us meat," the old man said. He sucked on the pipe and emitted a cloud of smoke.

The woman removed the bowls and went into the kitchen.

The boy used the medicine, a white salve, each morning and night, rubbing it lightly into the sores. Mornings and afternoons he often stood looking across the courtyard at girls playing nearby on swings and the village farmers in their fields and the old man and the woman working bent over and seeding the rice paddy and then plowing the second field and seeding it for millet. There were many birds in the fields and trees and he listened to their singing. Often huge dark birds circled overhead. Hawks.

On the night of the third day the carpenter looked at the boy's face and told him the sores were nearly healed. He was to use the medicine two more days and then return to the American compound. He had forgotten, he said, to tell the boy that if the Korean soldier asked him for money he was to say he would give it to him from his first wages.

"It is your gift to him for finding you this work," said the carpenter. "He will take only what is due him and no more."

"Remember to bring back meat," the old man said to the boy.

"Where do you think he will obtain meat?" asked the carpenter. "You think the foreigners give away meat?"

The boy woke that night thinking he had heard through sleep the sounds of weapons firing along the edge of the village. He lay awake trembling but all he could hear in the humid darkness was the breathing of the old man and the scurrying of mice across the floor.

Two days later the Korean soldier brought the boy again to the long low building and the American in the white coat looked at his face and wrote something on a piece of white paper which he gave to the soldier. The soldier took the boy across the compound to another long low building and as they entered the building the old woman, who was laundering clothes at the stream behind the village, felt a bubble of dizziness burst inside her head. She sat back on a flat rock and closed her eyes and envisaged the house burning and looked in terror over her shoulder. The house stood intact and tranquil. What was that? A vision sent by a fiendish spirit? Mother would tell me to quickly cook and eat some medicinal rice. But where can I find sugar now or honey or plums? She waited until the bad moment passed and the strange racing of her heart slowed and then went on with her laundering. When she was done she pulled the sleeves of her blouse over her reddened arms and wiped her hands and returned to the house carrying the laundry in a bundle on her head.

The chattering women on both sides of her and on the opposite bank of the stream had noticed nothing of her brief discomfort.

Before they entered the building the Korean soldier asked the boy, "Do you have the money?"

"I will give it to you from my first wages," the boy responded. The soldier seemed satisfied.

Inside the building was a long low-ceilinged room with many tables and chairs and a large end room with sinks and stoves and cabinets and boxes of food. A middle-aged Korean man in a white apron and a white cap stood at a table with a long-bladed knife in his hand. Lounging against a pile of potato sacks was a boy in his mid-teens, also wearing a white apron and a white cap.

"This is your new boy," the Korean soldier said to the man.

The boy lounging against the potato sacks made a low disagreeable snorting sound.

"You be quiet," the man said to him. "You shut your mouth, lazy bedbug." He turned to the boy. "You work hard?"

The boy nodded, his throat tight and dry.

"You work hard, you can work here. You don't work hard, out you go."

The other boy yawned.

"When you going to get rid of him for me?" the man asked the Korean soldier, pointing the knife at the teenage boy.

"I got you another boy," said the soldier. "Don't make trouble."

He went out.

The man looked at the boy. "Do you know what this place is?"

The boy shook his head.

The man said, "Listen, I'm the cook here, when I talk to you, answer in words."

"No," said the boy.

"This is a medicine-and-doctors battalion, where they bring the wounded and the sick. And here is the place where the officers eat. What is your name?"

The boy told him.

"What is your village?"

The boy told him.

"You are far from your village."

"My village is burned. Everyone is dead."

The cook and the teenage boy regarded him in silence.

"Everyone dead," the boy said. "Grandfather and Mother and Father and sisters and brothers and and uncles and aunts and friends and Badooki my dog is gone and and and everything is gone."

The cook and the teenage boy were very still.

"I don't want to talk anymore about my village," said the boy.

The cook closed and opened his eyes. After a moment he said, "All right, I will talk to you about cooking. Perhaps you will learn something. This lazy bedbug over here refuses to learn."

The teenage boy grinned.

"Do you know how to peel a potato?" the cook asked the boy. "I will teach you."

"Teach him how to peel an onion," the teenage boy said.

"Get out, get out," the cook said, waving the knife. "Go take care of your dirty business."

The teenage boy laughed and went from the kitchen.

"He is worthless to me," the cook said to the boy. "But for certain reasons I must keep him. Now we begin. Are you well? You look sick. Where do you live?"

"The village on the other side of that hill."

"With whom do you live?"

"Farmers, an old man and a woman who found me when I was hurt."

"They feed you and let you live with them? Very kind people. The kind ones you can count on the fingers of your two hands and your toes. I will give you something to take home to them. But you must work hard for me and not be like that lazy bedbug of a thief."

The boy peeled potatoes and onions and shelled peas and learned to set the tables and that evening served the meat platters, moving invisibly among the officers, and at the end of the day the cook seemed satisfied and gave him a gift. When the old man saw the gift he stared at the boy in astonishment and when the carpenter smelled the smoke of the gift he came hurrying into the house and the old man gave him a piece of the gift and they sat chewing and eating and looking at the boy from time to time, and the old man said to himself: This boy must not leave me, this boy is touched by the spirits, this boy has good power.

As the woman savored and slowly chewed and swallowed she wondered if the meat would remove the discomfort and heat inside herself. In the morning to her joy she felt well and as the boy walked to the compound she went off to the fields with the old man.

The boy worked for some weeks in the kitchen, peeling potatoes and learning to cook eggs and vegetables and meat and serving meals and every morning mopping the floor of the officers' dining room. On occasion the teenage boy would show up and the cook would send the boy from the kitchen and the two of them would talk quietly. Sometimes the cook would raise his voice at the teenage boy and call him a bedbug and a nest of lice and the teenage boy would laugh as he scurried from the dining room.

In the late spring the surface of the main road was an inch of yellow dust that traffic kept plowing and throwing into the air; it coated the buildings and tents of the compound and crept like dry mist into noses and mouths. Storms of dust rose and fell with the arrival and departure of hospital helicopters. The teenage boy appeared one day and offered to sell the boy a face mask that would protect him from the dust and the lung sickness, only the boys who got their jobs through him could obtain the face mask, did the boy want shadows on his lungs and not to be able to work. The boy bought the mask for a week's wages and wore it whenever he walked to and from the battalion compound but it did little good and he still tasted the dust on his tongue and deep in his throat.

The planting was done but the rains were late and the water in the channels was not enough for all the fields. The woman felt a curse was now blanketing the land: the fiends of war and drought had been set loose and were slaying the just and the unjust alike. Dust without end and the rising shimmer of heat over the fields and strange hot winds from the south. A shadow covered the sun and sometimes took the form of a winged creature. She saw it as she worked in the fields: a vast ugly furry creature, wings slowly rising and falling. Father to the creatures in the cave? No, those were good spirits. Good spirits of the earth and sky, good spirits of the valleys and hills and caves, end the war and bring the rains. Standing in the paddy, she paused in her work and made the vertical and horizontal motions of the cross. *Have thine own way Lord have thine own way.* Mother taught me.

Later she squatted by the stream over the laundry, her arms in the cool shallow water, and thought of the boy. At that very moment the boy was listening to the Korean soldier talking to him in the kitchen about another boy, who had worked cleaning the little houses of the officers and had not been to the compound for many days and seemed to have vanished. Did the boy want to take his place, the job was for more money than he was getting in the kitchen.

The boy looked questioningly at the cook.

"Stealing one of my best boys," the cook said to the soldier.

"What do you say?" the soldier asked the boy.

"Take it," the cook said.

The boy hesitated.

"Better than peeling potatoes and washing dishes and floors," said the cook. "You come in and visit, I give you something."

The boy nodded.

"Then it's done," said the soldier.

"You should go to school," the cook said to the boy.

"Don't give him fancy ideas," said the soldier.

"You're a smart kid. You should go to school and learn something. You want to spend the rest of your life here?"

"When you come in tomorrow, I'll show you what to do," said the soldier. "You got to pay me again for this new job, but don't worry, I'll take it out of your wages."

"Don't forget to visit," said the cook. "But meantime you're still working for me, finish those vegetables."

That evening the boy told the old man and the woman about his new job. The old man asked immediately, "The meat, what about the meat?" and the boy told the old man what the cook had said and the old man drew in on his pipe and gave the boy a nod of satisfaction. The woman said to herself: He is a boy doing the work of women. Let the war end so new work will begin. Let the rain come. Let there be an end to the shadow over the sun.

Later the old man went with the carpenter to the nearby town and the woman cleaned the bowls and lay down in her little side room to sleep. It was dark outside and cool and the boy stood in the courtyard breathing the pungent smells of the paddies and listening to the sounds of the village—night air in the trees, quiet voices from nearby homes, soft giggly laughter of girls—and the darkness seemed to him suddenly immense and vibrant with movement. The dead were scratching against the thin curtain that separated them from the living. He heard his mother calling to him and quickly reached out an arm—upon emptiness. Was that Father? Foolish boy, why are you living with farmers? And Grandfather's whispered response: Foolish? Where else is he to live? Look at him. What separates him from the orphans roaming the fields and streets? The confused mind of an old woman, the hungry belly of an old man, and an occasional piece of meat. A fragile bamboo reed upon which to hang one's life. They stood around him talking softly: Grandfather, Mother, Father. He reached out a hand to his grandfather and touched something and saw dimly by the light of stars the side of the cart. All the weeks with the cart then rushed back to him; this cart, this dumb assemblage of wood used by Grandfather and Mother and Father to help keep me and the old man and woman alive through seashore and cave and mountain and plain. Do Grandfather and Mother and Father hold such power even though they have no graves I can honor? Perhaps make a grave for them somewhere. Honor them all together. How?

A rush of wind in the tree startled him. He stood for some moments longer listening to the night and then returned to the house. He was asleep when the old man stumbled into the room and struggled out of his clothes and lay back on his pad and began immediately to snore.

The snoring woke the boy. Unable to sleep, he rose and took his pad and quilt and went out into the courtyard. He put the pad and quilt on the cart and slept there and woke chilled by the early-morning air. For a moment he was in the shanty on the plain and the flames had died in the firepit and the girl stood silhouetted against the snowy light motioning to him soundlessly to help her carry away her dead father. He lay shivering in the chill darkness and after a while climbed down from the cart and went back into the house.

The boy worked in the little canvas houses—Jamesways, he learned they were called—of the officers, making the beds, sweeping the plywood floors, wiping down the plastic windows, filling the five-gallon water cans, keeping the fire alive in the potbellied oil stoves; he did those chores day after day in the four small dim Jamesways assigned to him by the Korean soldier; and the old man and the woman harvested the rice crop in the burning heat and spread out the plants beneath the sun for drying.

As the rice lay drying the rains came and the old man and the woman worked to save the harvest. But much of it rotted in the torrents that poured from the sky and down the mountain slopes and through the gullies. The river rose and the stream behind the village flooded and the earth in the valley and foothills began to move and paths along which men had once safely walked with brushwood on their A-frames were now deadly with mines that had shifted with the sliding mud. The boy saw ambulances bring two old men to the battalion with their legs gone, and one of the girls from the village he remembered swinging up and down in a nearby courtyard higher and higher and giggling went off to play with friends of her chronological age on a hillside and stepped on what looked like a rock and vanished in a dull thumping noise and a rain of dust and pebbles and a spray of red mist. The rain tore away part of the grass roof of the old man's house and the carpenter and the old man labored to rebuild it, and the day they worked on the roof the boy went over to the officers' dining room to speak with the cook and the cook smiled and nodded and gave him another gift. The teenage boy was there and said idly, "How does the captain like his new phonograph?" and the boy said, "He plays it all the time," and the teenage boy said matter-of-factly, "Where does he keep it?" and the boy told him.

Two mornings later the captain woke and saw the cut in the canvas wall of the Jamesway made silently during the night right up against the dresser on which the phonograph had sat. The boy, when he heard of it, felt his heart surge with fear.

The next day the teenage boy tried to give him money and he refused to accept it.

The teenager said, "Listen, don't be a jerk. You think it bothers these rich foreigners? They have so much money they don't know what to do with it. Take the money. You do me more favors like that, you can save it all up and one day buy your old people an ox, I know what they are and where you live, don't play bigshot with me, you know what we do to fancy bigshot people here."

He turned and walked away, leaving the money in the hands of the boy.

That night the boy waited until the old man went out to the town with the carpenter and the woman was asleep. He dug a hole in the earth of the shed where the old man's ox had starved to death and put the money in a clay jug and buried the jug and covered it.

From time to time in the weeks that followed he would take out the jug and put more money into it and replace it, and sometimes he thought: Are the spirits watching me and what are they thinking, but it is for the old ones, how they work in the fields and the woman with the harness around her shoulders, it is unbearable to see her pulling the plow like an ox, and do the foreigners really care, they are so rich and fat. But spirits haunted him, he sensed them everywhere, and during the heat and dust of the late summer he woke often in the night and listened to their whisperings and sometimes he took his pad outside and slept in the courtyard and once even on the cart.

One night the woman woke and saw him by moonlight emerging from the shed and thought she was inside a dream until he stumbled and fell noisily and she called out to him and he said he couldn't sleep for the heat and the flies and had taken a walk by the stream.

Later he lay in the darkness listening to the old man snoring and thought of the officer who had arrived at the battalion that day, pale skin and red hair, they came and went and new ones took their places and they brought with them things, so many things, and they purchased new things, so many new things, doctors most of them, and a man who tended to their spirits, a man called chaplain who worked in the long white-painted building with the white cross on its tower.

The woman seemed interested in the chaplain. "Does he sing?" she wanted to know.

The boy said, "I have not heard him sing."

"Tell me if he ever sings this song," she said and sang for him in her quavering voice *Have thine own way Lord have thine own way thou art the potter I am the clay*.

The boy asked her what the words meant.

"Once I knew," she said, embarrassed. "But I have forgotten. It is the language of the foreigners."

The old man, who was sitting nearby smoking his pipe, said they were giving him a headache with all the talking and singing, he was going to the town with the carpenter, and he got to his feet and went out.

"He drinks as if there is still the black smoke," the woman said.

"The foreigners drink a lot," said the boy. "The cook says they drink to forget they are far from their homes."

"This man also has a lot to forget. He said to me you bring him memories." She was silent a moment and then she said, "I think he has begun to care for you. He hides it from you but he said to me two three days ago if you were our son he would make the hat ceremony in a few years and we would begin to look for a wife for you."

The boy felt his face burning.

"You are growing into a man but you are not our son and there is nothing we can do," the woman said and got to her feet to go into the kitchen. "You will tell me if you hear the foreigner singing those words. Perhaps he will explain to you what they mean."

But the boy never heard the chaplain sing that song. When the fall and winter came the war was still being fought in the north somewhere and there was famine in the village. Some of the old people died and the mournful cry "Aigo, aigo" was heard. The carpenter made their coffins and climbed about on the hills near the village measuring distances with his special instruments to determine the proper sites for their graves.

There were many blizzards and fresh snow fell upon old snow and crippled the roads and made it difficult to climb the hills for brushwood. The wind blew without end from the north, freezing the snow to ice, and the ice turned black and lay thick on the fields and paddies and hung like glittering dark knives from the roofs.

In the battalion the small dingily lit Jamesways on occasion reminded the boy of the cave in the valley. Sometimes alone in a Jamesway polishing an officer's boots he would fall into a reverie and see his grandfather and mother and father and once he saw Badooki and so clearly heard his barking he called out to him to be still he would disturb the doctor sleeping in the nearby Jamesway who had been up through the night in the hospital. On occasion the teenage boy would appear and they would talk briefly, and the gifts of food the cook gave him kept the old man and the woman alive that winter: and I am very frightened, what if I am caught; and the power of the boy is very strong, see what he brings us from the foreigners; and the man treats him like a servant, but I see the man's face I see his eyes I know that old man, he feels something for the boy.

The winter went on into spring and the ice took a long time to thaw. And when finally it was the time for plowing the boy went to the shed and removed the jug and in the presence of the woman gave the money to the old man and said it was for an ox, and after a brief moment of open-mouthed astonishment and a long knowing silence the old man nodded and took the money and together with the carpenter went to the nearby town. Several hours later they returned with an ox.

The village gathered around the ox: young and strong and sleek and tawny. Proudly the old man led it by its nose ring to the shed. The next morning he attached the ox to the plow and, speaking to it, took hold of the shaft. He guided it through the flooded paddy and felt upon his back the envious glances of the others in the fields.

All that spring the old man used the ox. When he did not need it for himself he rented it to others and with the money bought seed and food. Often the woman, while cooking in the kitchen or doing the laundry by the stream, would ask herself: Where does our good fortune come from? The boy is with us now a year and a half, does it come from him? Can that be the reason the man wants him to stay?

A new officer arrived in the late fall and the teenage boy appeared one day and asked the boy where the officer kept the new shortwave radio he had recently purchased in the post exchange and the boy refused to tell him. The teenage boy scowled but said nothing and went away.

A few days later, the radio disappeared. The boy was frightened he would be blamed but the officer bought another and locked it in his footlocker whenever he left the Jamesway.

Late one afternoon the boy went in to see the cook and the cook said there was too much stealing going on in the battalion, didn't the boy see the guards were now patrolling the fence with dogs and from today on everyone leaving the compound would be searched at the guardpost and at night there would be oil drums lighting the perimeter, he couldn't give him any more gifts of food. But the old man seemed not to notice the boy was no longer bringing food; the woman was able to buy dried fish and potatoes and some meat from the marketplace with the money earned by the ox.

In the spring they plowed and planted and one day in the summer they heard the war had ended but nothing in their lives changed, and one night in the fall, as the old man sat in the town drinking with the carpenter, he wondered silently if the border between the two lands might one day soon be opened so that he could go hunting in the North one last time before he died; but he did not think so. He asked the carpenter if he thought the boy would ever go hunting in the North and the carpenter, who knew of the old man's memories, said all things were possible for the spirits, and the old man bought the carpenter another drink of rice wine.

One winter afternoon the woman was washing clothes in the stream, bent forward over the cold water, and noticed her face in the dappled lights and shadows on the water surface. Old and ugly. *Have thine own way Lord.* It occurred to her that the stream probably emptied into the river and the river ran down the valley and through the big city and emptied into the sea and the sea returned to land somewhere as a river and the river became many streams that emptied into a river that flowed into a sea. And if my spirit enters the stream it will live on and on in the rush and drift and currents of its water. I will be the water and the riverbank and the cave and the mound on the plain. As she looked into the stream she saw the spirits of the water dark and coiling, and to her surprise they reached up and gently drew her to them, and she slid face forward into the stream and was pulled out by the women near her and carried to the house.

When the boy returned that evening he saw the old man and the carpenter in the house and the old woman beneath her quilts barely breathing, her face the color of parched earth, one eye open and the other closed. He sat on the floor near the woman and waited, making himself small, very small.

She died during the night.

In the early morning, when they were certain she was dead, the carpenter left to build the coffin and the old man took the woman's blouse and skirt and went outside and threw them onto the grass roof and called out her name. He then threw rice onto the roof and returned to the house.

The boy saw him sit down next to the woman and heard him begin to wail, "Aigo, aigo." He sat listening to the wailing of the old man, his heart frozen.

Soon two women entered the room and sent out the old man and the boy and began to ready the woman for burial.

The boy wondered if he should prepare food but he was very tired and not hungry and the old man seemed shriveled with grief. And so they sat in silence in the main room until the carpenter appeared with a compass and certain other instruments and talked awhile quietly with the old man as the boy wandered about the courtyard and from time to time came over to the cart and stared at it and touched it, the wood bitter cold in the suddenly icy winter air.

The carpenter came out of the house: a small white-bearded old man wearing a white coat and wadded white pants and a white cylindrical hat. The boy watched him go off in the direction of the hill behind the village.

Some minutes later the two women emerged from the house and went past the boy without a word. When the boy returned to the house he saw the old man staring in bewilderment at the lined leather gloves the two women had found in the chest where the woman had stored her few belongings. He handed the gloves to the boy.

"Go to your work," he said. "There is nothing for you to do here."

The boy had thought the gloves were lost; he could not remember when he had last seen them. There came abruptly to his memory the girl with the gray woolen gloves and carrying the body of her father and the vast pile of grotesque dead. Why had the old woman kept them? Holding them to herself. The boy's brown musty fur-lined leather gloves.

As he left the house he saw the distant figure of the carpenter scrambling about on the hill, pausing, gazing up at the ice-blue sky, measuring distances with an instrument, moving in straight lines and circles along the shoulder of the hill.

A new officer arrived that day, a troubled dark-haired man in his mid-twenties, to take the place of the previous one they called chaplain. The boy watched him unpack and carefully arrange his books in an old wooden fruit crate set on its end and now used as shelves in the Jamesway. Three orderly rows of books. Grandfather's books stacked book upon book on shelves in his little house off the courtyard. Odd how this chaplain did not have a cross on his collar but a kind of arching double tablet. Will he know *Have thine own way Lord*?

When the boy returned to the village in the evening the old man told him the carpenter had completed the coffin.

"And the grave?" asked the boy.

"The proper location for the grave is on the shoulder of the hill near the village."

"That is a good place," said the boy.

"But the cold has frozen the ground and our shovels cannot dig out the earth."

The boy felt a deep and terrible shuddering.

Inside the eyes of the old man were shadowy images of frozen bodies and fire and rising black smoke. Let the boy use his power for this.

Next morning the boy walked hurriedly to the battalion and spoke with the cook. In the early afternoon the teenage boy appeared at the door to the Jamesway where the boy sat polishing boots.

"You bring out the shine in those boots all right. The cook said you wanted to see me. What's it about?"

The boy told him about the grave and the frozen earth.

The teenage boy grinned and said, "You came to the right guy, but first you got to do something for me, you got to promise me something."

Shortly before the boy returned to the village a man appeared at the house and left a pickax with the old man. It was theirs to keep, he said.

In the early morning the old man and the boy climbed to the shoulder of the hill. Taking turns with the pickax and the shovel and the leather gloves, they began to dig the grave. Grinding hacking labor with the pickax and shovel through nearly eighteen inches of frozen earth until they reached free soil, still compact enough to need the pickax but without the wrenching force.

That afternoon the burial procession of the woman left the village and proceeded slowly along the path to the shoulder of the hill. The boy was among those who carried the coffin to the grave. Village women wailed. The boy watched shivering as men heaped earth onto the coffin and the grave filled. A cruel and evil wind blew across the hill and the blue sky seemed as frozen as the ground. From where he stood he was able to see the battalion and the long low building with the white cross and the Jamesway of the chaplain. He looked away and saw the old man holding open over the grave a small box and he heard the old man call out the woman's name and he saw, he was certain he saw, a gray shadow leap from the grave into the box. The old man closed the box and they all filed back down the hill. The old man carried the box into the house and placed it near the box containing the spirit of his father and covered it with a white cloth and sat down before it, silent, his eyes closed.

The following morning the boy prepared food for the old man and himself and offered it to the spirit of the woman by leaving it for some moments before the box. They ate the food and the boy cleaned the bowls and afterward climbed the hill and stood before the new grave. A low mound of earth. He tried to imagine the woman's face in the earth and saw instead the face of his mother. "Amuni," he murmured. Earth in her eyes and mouth and the village burning.

The new officer, the chaplain, was enraged: he had waked to discover his tape recorder gone. The boy could understand a little of what he overheard the officer telling the other officers. The tape recorder a farewell gift from his woman friend. Find the crooks who did this. From now on sleep with a bayonet under his pillow. The man's anger frightened the boy. Never do this again, never. Very dangerous now.

That night the boy cooked supper for the old man and himself and again offered it to the spirit of the woman. In the morning he climbed the hill to the grave. "Amuni," he murmured, addressing the woman, and realized it was also to his own mother he was now speaking. And he heard himself then say, "Grandfather, Father," for he saw them all here now in the grave of the woman.

This he did every day for the next week.

One day the old man saw him put on the wide hat of mourning and climb to the grave and return and leave the hat behind when he went off to the foreigners. The old man would not wear the hat of mourning: one did not wear it for one's wife, because a wife can be replaced but a father and mother are forever lost. Yet the old man felt keenly the loss of the woman, because suddenly there was no one to cook for him or wash or mend his clothes, and if it were not for the boy cooking what would he do; and he was also haunted by clear memories of the woman, and her voice was in his ears, and he could see her face when she was young and not yet ugly; and why had he not married again when it had become clear she could not bear children; had there been something in his feelings toward her deeper than the mere convenience of marriage? Now the spirit of the woman seemed to be everywhere around him, even when he went to the town with the carpenter to forget his sorrow, and one morning, as he watched the boy climb the hill to the grave wearing the hat of mourning, he felt deep within himself a slow and tortuous turning and then an opening of doors to deeper and deeper recesses inside himself, caves leading to caves, and his heart raced and he wondered if this was what was meant by the word love, which he had heard spoken from time to time, this baffling sensation of trembling warmth and closeness he now felt for this boy, and of course he said nothing of it to the boy and not a word even to the carpenter.

Weeks went by and every day the boy climbed to the shoulder of the hill in his hat of mourning and stood before the grave of the woman and his grandfather and mother and father. Sometimes he sang the song the woman had taught him, *Have thine own way Lord have thine own way*, and made over the grave the vertical and horizontal motions. Always he spoke to the spirits of the woman and his grandfather and parents, telling them of his work for the foreigners and his life with the old man and once even asking aloud if this was where he would spend all the rest of his years, was there nothing else he could do. If there is something else I can do, show it to me. Sometimes he woke during the night trembling with dreams and lay in the darkness and felt washing down from the hill the comforting spirits of the grave.

The teenage boy kept showing up at odd times. He seemed to know all the boys who worked in the battalion and many of the American sergeants. Once the boy saw him in a soccer game played in clouds of dust on the battalion compound during the first warm week of spring. Later the teenage boy came over to him, grinning and smelling of sweat.

"You be a help to me, I be a help to you," he said. "You got your ox and your pickax, you want something else big, you help me, I help you. You don't help me, I get another boy, boys like you everywhere, under every stone, think about it."

He went off and returned later that day. "Where does your officer keep the camera he just bought? I split with you half half, more than before."

The boy shook his head and remained silent and the teenager walked away.

Some days later a strange stirring was felt in the compound, and excitement played through the air. The boy sensed its presence and went to the cook.

"Ah, the battalion is moving to a new place," said the cook.

The boy was frightened. "Why does it move?"

"Too much dust from the road all the time, gets into the hospital, bad for the sick people."

"Will I lose my job?"

"I don't know about that."

"Does it move far away?"

"No, no, it moves only to there," said the cook and pointed through the wide window of the dining room to the hill behind the village.

The boy felt the lurching of the ground beneath him.

That evening he hurried back to the village and found they all knew: the carpenter had been informed by one of his acquaintances in the local administrator's office. The foreigners would soon be moving to the shoulder of the hill. Yes, the carpenter said somberly, the location of the old woman's grave would have to be changed.

"Where?" asked the boy.

"To the other side of the hill," said the carpenter.

"That will bring bad fortune," said the boy, trembling.

"Use your power to stop them," said the old man loudly.

The boy stared at him.

"You will know how to stop them," said the old man. "You saved the village, you brought us food, you found money for the ox." There was a tone of desperation in his voice. "Your strong spirits will protect the grave."

Even the carpenter looked with hope at the boy. And the boy stared back at them in astonishment and suddenly understood the reason the old man had let him remain with them in the village; and at that precise moment the old man, gazing at the boy's fearful and fragile face, his astonished eyes and trembling chin, realized he truly and deeply loved him. But he did not know what to say or do, and so he said and did nothing.

In his broken and halting English the boy spoke to the chaplain the next morning. "Battalion move to hill, sah?"

The chaplain looked surprised. He had been in the battalion some months and had never heard the boy say anything:

he always came and went silently, making himself small. "Where did you learn to speak English?"

"I listen American soldiers, sah. Soldiers say to move grave, sah. Not good place. Bad for amuni. Very bad for village."

"Calm down. Take it easy. What are you talking about?"

"Amuni grave on hill."

"What?"

"Amuni, sah. Mama-san. Amuni do for us good things. Amuni have nice place for grave and see all to the south. Now bad people come to village, sah. Bad men, bad women."

"What village?"

"Village near hill where I live. Bad people come make money from Americans."

"Well, I'm sorry, there isn't anything I can do. How old are you?"

"I thirteen almost fourteen, sah."

"Why aren't you in school?"

"No money, sah. No school. Grandfather great scholar and poet, but war come and village burned and everyone dead and I live with farmer in this village."

He saw the chaplain's face grow sad and dark, as though disturbed by a long-forgotten memory.

"I can't help you about the grave," the chaplain said and turned away.

The boy spoke to another of the officers, a doctor, who listened and asked, "Why are you so worried about the grave if she's not your real mother?"

"Spirit of my mother in grave too, sah. And spirit of my father. And spirit of my grandfather. All in same grave. Have no other grave."

"I don't understand. It's a good move to that hill. Get rid of this stinking dust."

Two days before the spring plowing the old man and the
boy and the carpenter brought the cart to the shoulder of the
hill, the old man and the carpenter on the shafts and the boy
pushing from behind. They opened the grave. The old man
would not let the boy look into the grave as he and the carpenter removed the coffin and loaded it on the cart and covered it
with canvas. They brought the cart to the slope on the other
side of the hill and with the boy looking away buried the old
woman again in the new grave they had earlier dug. Then they
returned to the village and that night after supper the old man
went to the town with the carpenter and the boy slept in the
courtyard on the cart and did not waken when the old man
returned.

One of the boys about his age who worked for the officers
vanished. They had become friends and he asked around for
him but no one seemed to know anything.

A second boy returned after a week away, his face purple
with bruises, but he would not respond to questions about his
absence.

During the time of plowing a new house was quickly
built along the perimeter of the village and four young women
moved into it. They lounged about in the courtyard and the
boy passed them on his way to the compound and returning
to the village, each time feeling the new stiffness in his groin,
and at night foreigners came to the house and the boy heard
their music and laughter. All the villagers knew this was the
end to their village, and the old man and the carpenter knew
this was the end to the power of the boy, his power could not
defeat the power of the foreigners.

One day during the time of planting the old man looked
up and saw flatbed trucks carrying huge machines across the
fields of wild grass between the battalion and the hill, and soon

bulldozers with big tracks and blades and tractors with claws that dug ditches were cutting and grading the hill. They come with their machines and their iron hearts, the foreigners, and change the face of the world. Change and death and more change and more death. Do the spirits change? Is there new death and new life and new death and new life among the spirits as well?

In the weeks that followed, the machines changed the shape of the hill: the shoulder was broadened and flattened; a wide road appeared; and deep drainage ditches and new long low white buildings with red crosses on the roofs.

When the first rains came the drainage ditches flooded and some of the houses slid off the hill but the machines pulled the houses back up and then dug the ditches deeper and soldiers lined them with stones. New houses appeared in the village too, and more girls, and men who were strangers opened little shanty shops that sold food and clothes, and uniforms and boots stolen from the foreigners.

One morning in the early fall the teenage boy entered the battalion compound and came over to the boy.

"Listen," he said, "soon we going to move to that hill. Either you're with me or you're my enemy. If you're my enemy you won't work in the new place. If you're with me you'll tell me where the officer keeps his camera. I've heard about that camera, it is something very special."

The boy did not respond and the teenager went away. But he returned in the afternoon.

"Listen, when we move to the hill I'm going to let you help me bring the foreigners to that new house in the village, because I hear you're smart and I need your English. It's my house, I run it. The most money is made from that and I'll see you get your share. If you don't want to do it, tell me and I'll get someone else. What do you say? Think about it."

He went away and was back the next morning.

"It's bad for my business if word gets out that one of my boys won't listen to me. I can't let that happen, because then others won't listen. You understand? I want you to think about that."

Later that afternoon the boy spoke to one of the doctors. The doctor told him he was tired, he had been up half the night with emergencies, the boy should go see the chaplain.

The chaplain was in Japan on a religious retreat. The boy talked to the chaplain's assistant, a man in his early twenties, light-skinned, blond-haired, cheerful. He didn't know anything about jobs in Seoul. Why did the boy want to go to Seoul, for heaven's sake? Seoul was an awful place. The boy would have to wait until the chaplain returned in a couple of days.

That night the teenage boy moved into the village, into the house with the four young women. The next morning he appeared in the doorway of the chaplain's Jamesway as the boy was sweeping the floor. He watched for a while and said, "You want to do this the rest of your life, work for the foreigners like a woman, get old working for the foreigners? You work for me, you make money fast. You're a smart boy, I watch you all the time, speak English, learn quick, you'll make lots of money. What do you say?"

The boy was quiet.

"Listen. Are you listening? An ox can die. One minute alive, the next minute dead. You know that? And houses burn. You know houses burn."

The boy said, "The foreigner took the camera with him. When he comes back I'll tell you where he keeps it."

The teenager grinned. "Smart boy, smart boy."

The morning after the chaplain returned, the boy came quietly into the Jamesway and lit the stove and set out the water basin and woke him.

"I speak to you, sah?"

The chaplain rose to one elbow. "What time is it?"

"Time to get up, sah. I speak to you? You man know the spirits, sah."

"What?"

"You have power, sah, more power than anyone else. You help?"

The chaplain put his legs over the edge of the bed and sat up, staring at the boy.

"Someone can hurt me, sah. He bad man and can hurt me and also hurt abuji papa-san, he live in our village now, sah, I no tell you his name, because he can hurt me very bad, and and he want your camera, but I not give him where it is and and he can hurt me and abuji papa-san and I afraid and and and I want go somewhere, far away maybe, to Seoul maybe, to work to study, Grandfather big scholar and poet, want me go study and and and you help me, sah, you man of strong power and know the spirits, please, sah."

The chaplain sat very still, looking at the boy.

"Please," said the boy.

The chaplain said, "I'll have him arrested."

The boy trembled visibly. "Ah no, sah."

"Why not?"

"He have many friends, sah. They can hurt me very bad. They can hurt abuji papa-san. He say they kill ox and burn house. Fire, sah." Village burning and earth in the old man's eyes and mouth.

The chaplain got to his feet. "You say your father was a scholar?"

"Grandfather. Big scholar, big poet."

"What does that mean here, a scholar?"

They talked while the chaplain washed and dressed. The boy wondered again about the six-pointed-star double-tablet insignia he wore. They walked together to the white building with the cross on the tower.

That night the old man listened to the boy and finally cried out, "Selfish boy! You go away now to study? I am an old man. Who will cook for me? Who will wash and mend my clothes? And and how will I end my days alone? And where where where is your loyalty and thanks after all I have done to save you? And what will the spirit of the woman say to this? Who will tend her grave?"

The boy did not respond. Shall I tell him they will kill his ox and burn down his house if I stay? He will shout "A knife to them!" and "Death to them!" and perhaps tell the old carpenter and a war will begin between the old ones and the young gangs. And if I stay where will I work? Perhaps I can find work somewhere and make myself small so they will not find me. Will I live all my life small? Small when they burned the village. Small in the cave and on the plain. Small in front of the machine that sees inside the body lights and shadows. Small and again small and and again and and and again. No! Small I left behind in the smoke and fires on the plain. No more small.

He woke early the next morning and dressed and walked through the village and climbed the hill. Cold soft clean sunlit air. Silent buildings of the new compound waiting for occupants. Guards with dogs along the perimeter. Skirting the compound, he went on to the rear of the hill, boulder-strewn and thick with tall grass, and came to the grave of the old woman, a small mound with a simple stone marker. Birds played in the grass and in the sky overhead. A tree of crooked timber grew not far away, shedding the last of its leaves. He pulled away weeds that had grown on the grave and placed

upon it the wild flowers he had picked on his way up the hill.
He stood in front of the grave and saw before his eyes a single
face that was the face of the old woman and his mother and
his grandfather and his father. One face that was all their faces.
Eyes and noses and mouths one to another fused. And be with
me forever and guard me from evil spirits and protect me from
bad people and and bring me safely to a better place and and
and . . . His voice high and thin in the hushed morning air, he
softly sang the song of the old woman. *Have thine own way
Lord have thine own way thou art the potter I am the clay.*

He felt no response. There seemed a sadness about the
grave, a desolation in the spirits residing there. Are the spirits
as helpless as men? Perhaps there are no spirits anymore, perhaps the spirits were all killed by the war, and only emptiness
is left for us to fill. Emptiness. Menacing as the cave, towering
as the mountains, broad and icy as the plain. Is it toward that
emptiness that I am being led? Like the girl and her mother
leaving the shanty on the plain and walking toward the narrow
opening beyond the bodies—to where? Fill the emptiness—
with what? Help me, my dead village. Be a strength to me,
my forlorn grave.

After a while he started slowly down the hill. Some yards
down he turned and climbed back up to the grave and scooped
up two handfuls of its earth, which he put into the pockets of
his jacket. He returned to the house and in the kitchen emptied
his pockets into a clean jar that had once contained food given
him by the cook on the American compound. He screwed the
cap back on and left the jar on a shelf in the kitchen.

On the day before the officers of the battalion were to
move to new quarters on the shoulder of the hill, the old man
and the carpenter and the boy walked together to the train
station in the nearby town. The boy carried a bag containing
some meager belongings and his jacket and the lined leather

gloves the old man had reminded him to take along and the jar of earth from the grave.

"Perhaps your power will return to you in the city," the old man said, squinting in the sunlight. He did not have the words to tell the boy his feelings and he kept looking up at the blue autumn sky.

The carpenter handed the boy a piece of paper with the names and addresses of two people he knew in Seoul. "In a strange city it can be of help to know someone," he said.

"I wish to say something to you," said the old man to the boy. "I speak to you as if I were your father, though I am not your father, you are not of my blood. Seoul is very big and it is easy to lose one's way there. You should go straight to the place the foreigner told you. In that place you should work hard and obey those who are above you. Stay away from women of the street and from women in houses like the one in our village; such women will bring you illness and misfortune. Eat meat as often as you can, it will cause what lies between your legs to grow large and firm. This I learned from my uncle, who as I told you was a great hunter in the North. That is all I wish to say to you."

The station was crowded. People chatted and stood about waiting reasonably for the train. The old man watched the traffic on the main road. Machines and machines and machines. Better to be old and soon dead.

The train pulled slowly into the station, wheels and brakes grinding.

The boy bowed deeply to the old man and the carpenter. The old man turned his head away so the boy could not see his eyes.

The boy climbed aboard. It was morning and the train was not crowded. He found a window seat and put his bag on the rack over his head. The window was coated with yellow dust.

Sitting in the train, the boy looked through the window at the old man and the carpenter. They stood on the earthen platform, gazing at him solemnly. He waved and they waved back. Two men, old and ugly. Yet more comforting than the emptiness ahead. Be a help to me, little jar of earth.

Creaking and jerking, the train left the station.

The old man and the carpenter started back toward the village.

They crossed over the drainage ditch on the side of the main road. Walking along the road, the old man saw a bird high against the blue sky. Huge wings. Circling. In the market-place he bought a piece of beef he thought he would try to cook for himself that night. And afterward rice wine in the town with the carpenter. He would soon forget the boy. Too many memories very bad. The bird still circling A hawk. Wheeling and gliding and circling. Uncle's hawk a swift gray shadow crossing the narrow valley. Guide the boy through the brown land, hawk. From anger of spirits deliver him. Circling. And now soaring higher and and still higher And and and too soon and too quickly vanished.

A NOTE ABOUT THE AUTHOR

Chaim Potok was born and raised in New York City. He began to write fiction at the age of sixteen, was graduated with a B.A. *summa cum laude* in English literature, and earned a Ph.D. in philosophy from the University of Pennsylvania. An ordained rabbi, he served as an army chaplain in Korea for sixteen months, with, successively, a front-line medical battalion and an engineer combat battalion. He is the author of seven previous novels and of *Wanderings: Chaim Potok's History of the Jews*. His first novel, *The Chosen*, was nominated for a National Book Award and received the Edward Lewis Wallant Award. Another of his novels, *The Promise*, was given the Athenaeum Prize, and *The Gift of Asher Lev*, his most recent work of fiction, won the National Jewish Book Award. He and his wife have three children and live in Pennsylvania.

A NOTE ON THE TYPE

The text of this book was set in a type face named Bembo. The roman is a copy of a letter cut for the celebrated Venetian printer Aldus Manutius by Francesco Griffo. It was first used in Cardinal Bembo's *De Aetna* of 1495—hence the name of the revival. Griffo's type is now generally recognized, thanks to the research of Mr. Stanley Morison, to be the first of the old-face group of types. The companion italic is an adaptation of the chancery script type designed by the calligrapher and printer Lodovico degli Arrighi, called Vincentino, and used by him during the 1520s.

Composed by Crane Typesetting Service, Inc.,
West Barnstable, Massachusetts

Printed and bound by The Haddon Craftsmen,
Scranton, Pennsylvania

Designed by Cassandra J. Pappas